Prisoner of Evil

They all heard the far-off train whistle. Peter tried to get away from the burly workmen, but they were on him like a pack of wolves. A fist sent him reeling against the one called Hitch, who grabbed him by both arms.

"You ain't goin' no place, brat. Ain't no so-called law gonna help y'now. Law says we's nothin' but superstitious hillbillies. Well, maybe we is and maybe we ain't. We know there's gotta be a reason nobody ain't never gone over the Ridge and come back less'n he's maimed or mindless."

Again the wail of the train, coming closer.

"Hell, that train'd grind his guts to hash," said one of the men.

The idea seemed to please them all.

"An' ain't nobody gonna be able t'say it warn't a accident . . ."

THE SKY CHILDREN

A NOVEL BY
DONALD OLSON

AVON
PUBLISHERS OF BARD, CAMELOT, DISCUS, EQUINOX AND FLARE BOOKS

THE SKY CHILDREN is an original publication of Avon Books. This work has never before appeared in book form.

AVON BOOKS
A division of
The Hearst Corporation
959 Eighth Avenue
New York, New York 10019

Copyright © 1975 by Donald Olson
Published by arrangement with the author.

ISBN: 0-380-00427-5

All rights reserved, which includes the right
to reproduce this book or portions thereof in
any form whatsoever. For information address
Blanche C. Gregory, Inc.
2 Tudor City Place, New York, New York 10017.

First Avon Printing, November, 1975

AVON TRADEMARK REG. U.S. PAT. OFF. AND
FOREIGN COUNTRIES, REGISTERED TRADEMARK—
MARCA REGISTRADA, HECHO EN CHICAGO, U.S.A.

Printed in the U.S.A.

"Fanatics have their dreams, wherewith they weave
A paradise for a sect . . ."

The Fall of Hyperion

Part One

"Waitin' fer kinfolk, sonny?"

Peter nodded. He was back in the station at Plato Switch after roaming up and down the platform wondering what Brokenstraw itself could be like if this whistle-stop was the nearest "big town."

"Looks like they's gone an' fergot y'." As he said this, the man traded grins with the stationmaster, hunched over his telegraph key in a dirty-windowed alcove facing the tracks.

By now the panic of not being met had subsided, and Peter fingered his return ticket, pondering how soon he might be justified in using it. Ripples of homesickness were building into waves, and this hillbilly's ribbing didn't help. The lout kept spitting tobacco juice and giggling when he missed the spittoon, and there was something morbid about tattoos on such skinny arms. He finally wandered off, but to Peter's dismay was soon back with a bottle of orange soda pop.

"Wet yer whistle on this while y're waitin'."

It had a cold but oddly chemical taste. Peter hoped it wasn't drugged. (When the train trip had grown tiresome, he had converted it into epic myth by imagining he was a royal fugitive being hounded into exile.)

"Ain't Beau Bucklin's kin, by any chance?"

"No, sir."

"Wunnered. Brother's youngster's comin' in tomorrow. Thought there mighta been a mix-up."

He took a whack at a fly with his bare hand.

"Missed. Hey now, ain't that there a queer-lookin' doodad." He was grinning at the elaborate coat of arms Peter had painted on Daddy's old suitcase.

"Family crest," said Peter coolly.

"What's that there say? Non—"

"Non ignara mali."

Peter's interest quickened. "Our motto." Without being asked, he repeated the three words, rolling them off his tongue as grandly as an Italian tenor. "It means *Not unacquainted with misfortune*," he added.

The man laughed and asked him where it was his misfortune to be going. Had Peter been sure that Affie Juul would not momentarily show up and make a liar out of him, he might have answered "Abroad." As it was, he told the truth.

It had a most unexpected effect.

The look that came over the man's face at the mention of Brokenstraw clearly suggested he must have known all along why there had been no one there to meet Peter.

Joyfully, Peter welcomed visions of calamity: flood, fire, tornado, with poor Aunt Affie—and indirectly himself—among the victims; his visit would end before it began. He raised his chin and tried to look brave.

The man's response was anything but sympathetic. He crossed to the alcove and whispered something to the stationmaster. They both stared at Peter. The stationmaster reached for his telephone.

Peter had no idea what to make of all this, but there was no mistaking the venomous look on the skinny man's face when he came back.

"What's yer name, kid?"

"Peter Patrick."

"Yeah? Ain't never hearda no Patricks round these parts."

"I'm visiting my aunt."

The squint-eyed face came closer. "What's her name?"

"Juul. Actually, she's my great-aunt."

The man shot another look at the stationmaster.

"An' you figger she's gonna come across the Ridge fer y'?" There was a sly, malignant humor in his tone as he said this, and a sneering quality which made his face even uglier, more threatening.

Before Peter could answer they both heard the long, low tiger's purr of an approaching train, whereupon the man swore, aimed another wad at the spittoon, tramped out of the depot and across the tracks to grab up the mailbag flung from the passing train, tossed the bag into a pickup truck, and sped away in a cloud of dust.

Odd.

Trying his best to whistle, Peter moved toward the door,

half expecting the stationmaster to come after him, but just then a shiny black sedan came bouncing over the tracks and into the yard. The driver jumped out, looked quickly around, and hurried straight up to Peter.

"You Peter Patrick?"

Peter nodded. "Are you from—"

"Mrs. Juul."

He was one of those rare beings who measured up to Peter's bookish ideas of the heroic. For one thing, he had that earthy brown skin which Peter, who burned and peeled, regarded with such acute envy, the blood-brown ruddiness of a man in touch with the sun and soil; and instead of pale, slimpsy hair like a girl's, his was rough as raw wool and only a shade darker than his skin.

"Name's Krieg. Your stuff inside?"

Most names never quite fit; Krieg's was somehow perfect. Peter put out his hand, but Krieg seemed in too great a hurry to notice it—or the phony emblem on the suitcase, luckily. To utter something like *Non ignara mali* to a man like Krieg would sound hopelessly affected.

The depot's air of menace vanished with Krieg's arrival. Peter forgot the tattooed man and ignored the stationmaster's murderous glare. Hillbillies.

"What in blue blazes you got in here, sport?"

"Just my barbells." Here was something a man like Krieg would appreciate more than coats of arms and Latin mottoes. "Only the small ones. I work out with them every morning."

If Krieg could see no evidence of this in Peter's noodle arms and skinny shoulders, he was too courteous to say so. As for Peter, he was suddenly glad he'd come, already seeing himself at summer's end as brown and sinewy as the man beside him.

Wondering if Krieg knew why he was there, he said, "I'm not really sick, you know. I'm a lot stronger than I look."

All Krieg said was "Better make it snappy, sport."

Even more than Peter, he seemed eager to get out of there.

In the car, Peter tossed a last scornful glance at the village behind them, catching a glimpse of two men standing in front of the ramshackle general store; astonished, he saw one of them point in his direction and make an oddly threatening gesture. He was about to say something to

Krieg when he saw the same black pickup in which the tattooed man had driven away come jouncing down the village street toward them.

"Look!" he cried. Several men rode in the back of the truck, all of them brandishing clubs!

"Quick, sport. Roll up your window!"

Krieg raced the engine but didn't let out the clutch.

Out the back window, Peter watched the truck lunge past the general store and speed toward them. He looked frantically at Krieg, who was dividing his attention between the rear-view mirror and the tracks.

The signal flashed red.

"Krieg, step on it!"

Epic myth was one thing. This kind of royal send-off was something else. Move! Move!

But Krieg didn't move, not until the pickup swerved into the yard and Peter saw murder in a dozen eyes. Then Krieg stepped on the gas, but instead of bolting for the tracks as the pickup's driver plainly expected him to do, he made a sharp turn the other way, circled the station, and sped toward the street as though heading for the village. The pickup was thrown into reverse to block him off, but to Peter's utter disbelief Krieg swung the sedan hard to the right and gunned it directly in front of the truck and straight toward what appeared to be certain collision with the onrushing train.

Peter shut his eyes and froze for the impact.

The whistle shrieked, the planks in the crossing rumbled, the car swayed as if jostled by the edge of a howling twister.

Peter looked back at the moving wall of freight cars. Krieg was laughing.

"How's that for a rousing welcome, sport?"

"Who are they?"

"Bullies from Plato Switch."

Peter told him about the mail clerk.

"Sorry, sport. Train was early or I'd been there sooner."

"But why should they care about me?"

Krieg spoke vaguely about a local feud. Peter kept glancing back. "Shouldn't you go faster?"

"Don't worry. They won't come after us."

Nor did they. The winding dirt road into the piny hills was deserted. Krieg pointed out Brokenstraw Ridge ahead of them: a rocky, wooded barrier isolating Brokenstraw Valley from the rest of the countryside.

Rugged was the word for it, and wildly beautiful: pine forests rising out of pink-faded mountain laurel, sumac and sassafras; jagged outcroppings of pebble-studded limestone, boulders bigger than elephants; a dramatic landscape, unfamiliar enough to fill Peter with a dull foreboding and to bring on further waves of homesickness.

How appalled Mother would be to know what a wilderness she had consigned him to and what a welcome had awaited him. And all for the sake of his health!

A month ago, shortly after his fifteenth birthday, Peter had suffered what he thought was a mild heart attack while struggling one night in his room with a knotty proposition in plane geometry. The doctor had sounded his young patient's puny white chest, grunted musical words like *systolic* and *diastolic*, showed more interest in Peter's lungs than heart, and finally recommended he be removed from school for the rest of the term and sent into the country for the fresh air and sunshine not often enjoyed in their own Midwestern suburb.

Having almost lost their son during a scarlet fever epidemic, when reckless doses of belladonna—this was long before the age of penicillin—had nearly made a dope addict out of Peter, the Patricks had readily agreed. But as they had no close friends or relatives in the country, the advice might never have been acted upon if Peter's mother had not taken it into her head to appeal to his dead grandmother's half-sister, an almost legendary great-aunt named Affie Juul, who lived in a remote Appalachian village and about whom Mrs. Patrick herself had only the scantiest knowledge.

Although Mrs. Juul's reply to Mrs. Patrick's first letter was cordial enough, it had been politely evasive; and it was not until Peter's mother had proposed coming along, too, in order to relieve Aunt Affie—as she made a point of addressing her—of any extra work the visit might create, that the old lady had finally yielded—but only on condition that Peter came alone. Her purpose achieved, Mrs. Patrick took this rebuff in good humor, seeing nothing sinister in it, and within a week had put Peter aboard the train for Plato Switch.

Presently, in what appeared to be the fringe of the

forest on the other side of the Ridge, Krieg pulled off the road.

"Hungry, sport?"

"Yes!"

Krieg spread a blanket under the trees, unpacked the hamper: cold fried chicken, pickles and cheese, flaky yellow pastries oozing blood-red jelly, and a jug of milk.

Krieg said, "Take a snooze after, if you've a mind to."

Peter was often amused when elderly women took him for a much younger child; for Krieg to do so was mortifying. "Naps are for babies. I'm fifteen."

Krieg laughed. "I'm just shy of thirty, and I still take naps." He stood up and reached for the sky, and Peter thought how marvelous it would be to have a body like Krieg's, then and there swearing to double the number of his daily exercise routines.

"Finish off that grub, now," said Krieg. "I'm gonna stretch my legs. Not scared of bein' here alone, are you, sport?"

About to leap up, Peter decided to stay where he was.

Assuming Krieg was really only going out of sight to pee, Peter lay back and stared up at the schooner masts of pine trunks with their tightly furled green riggings, all becalmed among the pale cloud reefs of the summer sky.

How still it was, yet with something almost rhythmic in the stillness; he felt vaguely helpless, like a traveler alone in a strange land, surrounded by unseen creatures (an ant was journeying across the arch of his foot) who were closer to the earth than he had ever been, the earth of trees and birds and animals, of stones and rooted things, and yet who were nearer to the sun as well—it might have been caught up there in the crown of this nearest tree; and he was gripped by an alien's uneasiness in this swarming world, its language a mystery, its strange, slumberous, watchful silence too unsettling to be borne for long without making the listener edgy, like Mozart on a tin ear.

He struck a satirical, big-chested pose and said aloud, "Skip the crummy nap, *sport*."

His voice echoing among the pines gave him the willies, and he went looking for Krieg along the nearby brook where the water was so clear you could see every pebble on the bottom, and pink scuttling crabs trailing muddy veils, and schools of darting silver minnows.

In a tiny estuary where the water was like glass, he lay

on his belly and examined his face, pale and citified, with the green-filmed sky behind it, then jabbed the surface with one finger, his features wrinkling, growing old, dissolving.

Across the creek the ground was boggy, thick with the rank, ribbed leaves of skunk cabbage, cattails, and cowslips as glossy as buttercups.

A burst of laughter, quickly smothered, came unexpectedly out of the woods above him. He waited for it to be repeated; when it wasn't he quietly set out to explore the area beyond the creek, stopping very suddenly behind a fringe of trees at the edge of a shallow glade.

Sunlight shimmered on the naked bodies of a man and woman locked together on the ground.

The man was Krieg.

Once he'd taken in the bizarre linkage itself, he was eager to see more of the woman's body than its pale arms and legs wrapped around Krieg's thrashing haunches. Black hair spilled over the leaves, but her face was hidden.

Krieg's body, muscled from shoulder to calf, was no surprise.

He watched them pump and heave, sweating like wrestlers, the woman whimpering as Krieg mouthed her, until abruptly, as if a single bullet had instantaneously killed them both, all motion froze.

Peter held his breath, sure they must have heard something, yet Krieg took his time moving away from the woman, rolling over on his back, his chest rising and falling, one hand curled lazily over his crotch, the other fending off an invisible insect.

The woman's breasts were like limp, nippled, half-inflated balloons; not quite what Peter had expected. As Krieg stood up and started to dress, she raised herself on one elbow and Peter got a good look at her face. Neither she nor Krieg uttered a word.

Pretending to be asleep when Krieg returned to the car, Peter was surprised when he flopped down on the blanket beside him and immediately started snoring, his mouth slightly open upon the bright clean edge of his teeth, a faint slime of sweat lacing his upper lip. Though there was a boyish softness about his face in repose, he still looked as rugged as the Ridge behind them, an epic hero in an heroic setting. Peter, his admiration quickened if anything by what he'd seen in the glade, slipped off his shirt and braced his bare chest up to the sun, shutting his eyes and making a furious effort of will to be strong and brown like the man beside him.

Brokenstraw at sundown: a few doll-like shops, shady streets that were tunnels of coolness under what his grandmother had called "elmbrellas," where old white Greek Revival houses drowsed in clouds of azalea and honeysuckle.

Aunt Affie's was rather grander than Peter had expected: Corinthian pillars and a stained glass fanlight; his mother would have adored it, she was mad about "magnolia" houses. And the old lady on the porch—it might have been Gram herself, the same expansive face, furrowed and double-chinned but unruined by age, a twilight apparition made luminous by dusk, angel-eyed, ghostly.

She crossed the porch and kissed him with soft, cold lips.

Sleep pushed slowly into his overcrowded mind that night. In a room still decorated like a nursery except for a huge four-poster resurrected from some musty attic whose odors still clung to it despite the freshness of its sheets, he imagined he'd died at home, the doctor had come too late, found him already cold and stiff, and the trip he'd taken was into the land of death, with Gram to welcome him so he wouldn't be afraid.

And yet he was.

Once he must have dozed off because he was frightened awake by what he thought was a dream figure, until Aunt Affie, looming beside him with eyes that were oddly bright, like a night animal's, touched him with a cold hand.

"Can't sleep, darlin'?"

"No."

"Too tired. I'll bring you somethin'."

She drifted away and came back with a glass full of some warm, thick beverage.

"Drink it down, darlin'. Nothin' but honey and warm milk."

Whatever it was, it worked, and soon there were only patchwork dreams: bare bodies, tattooed breasts, black hair, smell of earth and pine needles, sweat and honeysuckle; his own lost room with its books and banners.

Waking in the dead of night, he heard whispering outside his door—or was it the wind in the chimney? His eyes picked out dim faces on the wallpaper: dolls, clowns, rocking horses; monsters from a stranger's past, watching him, hating him. Through white stirring curtains, a faint odor of sweet williams.

Somewhere in the house a girl was laughing.

"I'm a stickler for discipline, let me warn you, darlin'. I can be mean as a witch in a windstorm."

Her laugh, with its trace of brininess, sounded like something sloshing around in a very deep barrel. "No rambunctiousness! You're here to get well; don't you forget that."

"But, heck, I'm not really sick."

"That's your opinion. I've seen bonnier specimens in a pine box. Never mind. We'll send you home so plump and brown your own darlin' mama won't know it's the same boy. Go on, have another blackberry muffin."

She said that Welcome had baked them. "Later on, you can help her make a batch of rosettes."

Batches of rosettes sounded intriguing but faintly sissy, like some sort of fancywork.

"And Krieg will take you fishing, soon's he has time. We're all busy as bear cubs at fly time gettin' ready to move out to Sugar Hill." Her son Theron's farm, she explained, where she always spent the summer.

Krieg's status puzzled him. What fun if they were cousins; but she laughed at this and told him Krieg merely worked for the family, and then she gave him a long, considering look and said with the barest hint of reproach, "Any more questions, darlin'?"

"Is he married?"

"No, he ain't. Why do you ask?"

"Just wondered."

"He say he was?"

"No."

She looked pleased. "Krieg's a treasure, but don't let him pull your leg. Now finish your muffin and then you can go out and play. Only mind you don't go out of the yard."

Welcome had the reddest hair he'd ever seen, and the heart shape of her face with its white skin and pink bow lips made him think of valentines. She was jolly and quick and hugely, embarrassingly pregnant. Peter tried to dodge her belly while they made the rosettes. She let him hold the handle of the black iron mold, dip the mold into a creamy batter, then plunge it into boiling oil where the fluted edges formed a flaky, crispy rose, held just long enough in the oil to make it golden brown, then rolled in a bowl of powdered sugar until it looked like a big edible snowflake.

She made a joke of his clumsiness; he hadn't giggled so crazily in months. She was more like an engaging child than a pregnant woman and he felt for her, as he had for Krieg, an immediate glowing fondness. He noticed she wore no wedding ring and read into its absence shocking possibilities, one of them that Krieg was to blame for her big belly. In which case, what right did he have to be seducing dark ladies in the woods? He already hated that black-haired temptress. If she was Welcome's rival, she was his enemy.

Surely anyone in his right mind would rather kiss Welcome than that other creature. Those small, curved lips were kissing lips. He'd like to kiss her himself! And yet he supposed she'd as soon kiss another girl as him, and he felt annoyingly, hopelessly sexless, wishing he were as sturdy as Krieg, as tough and manly, instead of all kitcheny and clean.

Was Aunt Affie rich?

The clues were ambiguous. The house was big but not opulent, nor was there a hint of the grande dame about Aunt Affie herself; yet Krieg and Welcome must have been amply paid to serve her with such apparent loyalty.

Another question to which he could get no straightforward answer: Why were Aunt Affie and Welcome making such a fuss to impress the visitor coming to tea?

"Mr. Edward Breed's a very important gentleman, darlin', from the Abbey," is all Aunt Affie would say as she inspected his appearance for the tenth time.

Intriguing, but what was it—a school? Insane asylum? An *abbey?*

"You might bring your sketchbook down while he's here," she added. "It's the sort of thing would amuse him." She gave his collar a final tug. "And Miss Celestia, too."

This was the first mention of a woman visitor. "Is she coming, too?"

"Mercy, no. Miss Celestia never leaves the Abbey." He decided reluctantly it must be a school, then brightened as Aunt Affie made a discreet circle over her ear. An asylum, then?

He was watching from his window when a pearl-gray Packard, as shiny as Aunt Affie's Willys but sprinkled with yellow road dust, parked in front of the house and a young man in a black visored cap hurried to open the rear door, out of which stepped a moderately fat gentleman in a gray suit made of some lustrous material that glistened in the sun, as if the sweat he was mopping from his broad face had already oozed from his body and drenched the garment.

He was no more prepossessing when he sat in the parlor plucking an oval cigarette from a lizard case and tapping it on his beefy, hairless wrist.

One gets an impression of wounded vanity, of cynicism penetrating the skin but not quite reaching the soul.

This description of the visitor was confided to Peter's diary that night and, like most of its entries, was more literary than accurate.

Certainly his eyes did have brilliance without warmth, and though his coloring was as dark as Krieg's, he looked somehow more smoked than tanned. The few hairs languishing on the desert of his scalp looked as if they'd been carefully combed into place by a man whose last worldly illusion is that he's not as bald as his mirror testifies.

Conversation between Aunt Affie and the visitor was a tepid exchange of pleasantries: inquiries about Miss Celestia and a certain Dr. El by Aunt Affie, similar inquiries from Mr. Breed about the folks at Sugar Hill. She assured him, they were well. He reported Miss Celestia was "no worse." No mention of Dr. El. Whatever sort of doctor he might be, he could never have examined his patients with a more probing eye than that which Mr. Edward Breed kept directing at Peter.

Presently, Aunt Affie suggested Peter show their guest his sketchbook. Mr. Breed seemed less than fascinated, leading Peter to suspect once more that he must indeed be connected with a school and accordingly long since sapped of enthusiasm for such exhibits. Nevertheless, he politely gave his attention to the modest portfolio.

"And what, pray tell me, is this?" he asked.

"My family crest."

Mr. Breed turned an amused eye on Aunt Affie.

"My father's family," Peter added hastily.

"Indeed? Descended from a duke, I see. *Très grand*."

Realizing, too late, that Mr. Breed was not such a

dummy after all, Peter began to sweat. Who would have thought that anyone in Brokenstraw would know the significance of strawberry leaves on a coronet?

But there was worse to come.

"Non ignara mali, miseris succurrere disco." Mr. Breed bared his teeth in a savage, demolishing smile. "You see, I know my Vergil, young man, though that particular aphorism may be found in any dictionary of foreign terms."

Where you, my young scoundrel, undoubtedly found it, he might as well have added. Peter looked helplessly at Aunt Affie, who merely beamed and said nothing to rescue him.

Mr. Breed kept him on the spit. "How extraordinary to meet aristocracy in Brokenstraw. My brother will be charmed."

Peter stammered a clumsy denial of such connections. "I just think it's fun to copy historical things," he ended weakly.

At this point the visitor mercifully drew in his fangs.

"In that case you should find a visit to the Abbey most interesting. Don't you agree, Mrs. Juul? It's an exact replica of my ancestors' English country place, right down to a secret chamber where fugitive Cavaliers hid from the Roundheads."

Peter's embarrassment vanished. Furthermore, one couldn't entirely despise any man who could eat four of the powdery rosettes without spilling a trace of sugar on his tie or vest.

To his surprise, Aunt Affie suddenly told him he could be excused, and there was something in her tone—a peremptory note he'd never heard before—that silenced the protest he might otherwise have made.

Stung by such an abrupt dismissal, he crept back and listened at the door, curious to know what the two of them had to say that wasn't meant for his ears.

It was more than he'd bargained for.

His ear picked up the tag end of a remark from Mr. Breed:

"—say anything or do anything to make him suspicious."

Him?

Aunt Affie's reply was even more intriguing:

"With a watchdog like Krieg?"

"I've an idea he's rather slier than you think, Mrs. Juul."

"Krieg, or him?" A joke, apparently, for she sounded amused, and Mr. Breed chuckled.

In a more serious tone, she said something Peter couldn't make out.

"He's not an infant," replied Mr. Breed. "You mustn't forget that. It could be dangerous."

"But he'd have no reason to be suspicious."

"At that age they don't need reasons. If he were to say anything to them . . . in a letter—"

"Trust me," she said. "He won't. I promise."

"She's obviously an overweening type. And stubborn. If she were to sense even a whiff of anything—irregular . . . she might come rushing down here."

"No danger. I made it perfectly clear it could be only the *boy*."

Peter heard Mr. Breed's cigarette case snap shut. "The whole thing must be handled with the utmost delicacy, Mrs. Juul. I'm sure you understand that."

"But if Dr. El isn't willing . . ."

"Leave that to me. He'll come around."

For a moment or so neither of them spoke; Peter was ready to dash for the stairs. Then he heard Aunt Affie say, "What about her, then?"

"I thought of taking her now, but there's no point. As long as you're all coming over, you can bring her back with you then."

"Whatever you say. Lord knows, I can still use her."

"Gently, I trust."

"I always have."

"We'll have everything ready," he said.

"It's all such a chore," she whined. "I don't know why I bother."

"I, for one, shall breathe easier when you're settled out there," said Mr. Breed.

She laughed. "Oh, out there. Lord, yes, no problem there."

"One's vigilance mustn't be relaxed, Mrs. Juul. Even out there."

"Oh, I know that. I didn't mean . . ."

"Of course, of course." He added something in a lower voice, they both laughed, and then Mr. Breed started making sounds of departure.

For a boy with his inventive mind, it took him an unusually long time to make sense out of all this; it was not until late that night, in fact, as he lay in bed mulling it over that the pieces all slid into place.

It was all on account of the baby!

This is how he saw it: Krieg and Welcome were secret lovers. Welcome had begun to grow a baby, and Peter had read enough books to appreciate the fix of unmarried girls who got pregnant. Especially country girls. Mr. Breed was obviously Welcome's guardian. Peter discarded the idea of his being her father: the role of heartless guardian was more romantic.

Welcome must have been living at the Abbey when she met Krieg, perhaps while walking in the woods—met him and fallen in love with him and shared with him reckless trysts among the pines. Then the baby started; Mr. Breed had somehow found out. Maybe Welcome had gone around throwing up in the mornings, or fainting; in books, that was what usually put someone wise. There had been scenes, wild recriminations, oceans of tears, but Welcome had not betrayed her lover, and in the end she had been sent to stay with Aunt Affie in a condition of punitive servitude until she repented or until it was time for the baby to be born.

Then along had come Peter, an outsider. Aunt Affie had tried to discourage the visit until Mother, had virtually threatened to bring him herself, welcome or not.

Mr. Breed, dreading scandal, had made haste to inspect the intruder, had found him sly and taken pains to see that everyone kept him in the dark.

The flimsy logic of all this didn't trouble Peter, and details that didn't quite fit, like the dark lady, for instance, he explained away by granting Krieg couldn't help being the sexy fellow he was, a man for whom fidelity would be a physical impossibility, and scarcely even a virtue. And wasn't poetry and legend full of dark ladies?

Besides, what other explanation could there be?

There was no time for Peter to confirm his suspicions either by adroit questioning or cautious snooping. They were all too busy preparing to move to the farm, a task that could not have involved a greater number of niggling details if they had been leaving the country altogether.

Removing all the light bulbs, for instance—"to reduce the risk of fire," Aunt Affie explained—blandly disregarding Peter's insistence that pulling the plugs was quite sufficient.

A visit to the Abbey had been set for Sunday, the day before they were to move to the farm. Peter was sure that Welcome must have known she wouldn't be returning with them, yet her attitude was strangely unperturbed. In fact, she was so cheerful about the whole thing that he began to fear her mind wasn't all it should be. Not until they were in the car and on their way to the Abbey did he realize it was all a conspiracy.

It was for *his* benefit they were putting on this act.

If Welcome had been even mildly downcast, or if Krieg had shown the dimmest spark of rebellion, he wouldn't have been so hurt by this affront to his intelligence. But no, the act was perfect; they were all maddeningly polite. Krieg and Welcome grinned in the front seat while Aunt Affie calmly pointed out things of interest along the roads they followed, country lanes hemmed with dusty borders of Queen Anne's lace and ripening milkweed.

Peter was surprised not to see any of those tottery paintless farmhouses he always saw in other backwoods areas, inescapable as Mail Pouch tobacco signs; here the farms were all freshly painted, spacious, handsome and immaculate, more like his romantic picture of the antebellum South, not so much farms as plantations, so extremely neat he wondered if their owners were Dutch. Names on mailboxes gave no clues: Leeving, Callodene, Knoel.

The sun was tipping westward when they came to a break in the trees, an artificial lake, iron gates flanked by stone lions, and then the sort of park Peter had seen only in old engravings of European manor houses.

"Look for deer," said Aunt Affie, but he didn't have to; they grazed in plain sight, heedless of the car's passage. Presently the lane broadened, was paved with gravel. Peter leaned forward.

They were there, and his first thought was that it didn't belong in Brokenstraw Valley any more than he did: mullioned windows in a vast gray pile of ivied stone topped by a forest of Gothic chimneys.

Peter was charmed.

Then, guiltily, he looked at Welcome and saw not even the slightest trace of apprehension.

A man in a dark suit came out the front door and ushered them into the hall, a baronial cavern hung with oil portraits and boasting a fine replica of an Elizabethan staircase rising to a gallery bathed in the jeweled gloom of stained glass windows. Entranced, Peter gazed about him for several moments before realizing that he and Aunt Affie were alone.

"What happened to Krieg and Welcome?" he said, looking around.

"Ain't this somethin' to write home about, darlin'?"

"Yes, but where are Krieg and Welcome?"

"They're bein' looked after."

She stepped closer and he noticed for the first time that her nose, unlike Gram's, had a hook to it, making her eyes more hawkish than dovelike. Her manner was fidgety and her tone of voice nervously abrupt.

"You must stop frettin' about Krieg and Welcome, darlin'. They're quite happy, I promise you."

He thought this an extraordinary remark, but before he could reply, the familiar figure of Edward Breed, dignified somewhat by its Gothic frame, oozed out of the shadows. Peter thought there was an air of replication about him as well, as if, like the portraits and the very building surrounding him, he might have been a copy of some lost original.

He welcomed them with a formal smile and announced that Miss Celestia would receive them in the Long Gallery.

Along the way, Peter caught glimpses of a dark-paneled dining room, old silver, refectory table, X chairs; a library in faded rose-beige tapestry; a sitting room in green; an oriel window.

The Long Gallery itself was as vast as a hotel lobby.

Their hostess was at first invisible, lost at the far end of the room in a clutter of tables and sofas, chairs and ottomans, silk-shaded lamps and potted palms; moreover, Edward's courtliness and the mansion's splendor had prepared Peter for someone on the scale of the Athena of the Parthenon, not this wizened cripple sagging to one side in a wheelchair and peering up at them from under a mad fringe of webby hair.

Below the neck, shawls covered all but her matchstick arms. Peter guessed her to be ancient, much older than Aunt Affie, and he was struck by her brilliant eyes, so dramatically at odds with her general air of physical defeat.

When she spoke her voice rang out startlingly loud, then

faded to a whisper, so that one kept leaning toward her and then jerking back as if in continual obeisance to her shrunken figure.

Her frantic gaze fastened on Peter. "Why, isn't she a pretty little thing!"

Outraged, Peter felt the blood rush to his face.

"He, he!" cried Edward. She looked at him crossly. "What's *he* laughing about?"

Edward's pink sloppy lips pouted humorously. "Merely correcting your allusion to our young guest's gender, Auntie C."

"Don't bother." She stuck her tongue out at him. "I can see what she is."

Edward's yeasty smile implored Peter's patience. "*He* is a very gifted lad, Auntie C. Show her your sketches, young man. She used to be very fond of pictures."

Indeed, Peter might have been mollified by the rapt attention she gave to the first sketch had she not been holding it upside-down. No one said anything. Handing it back, she looked at Aunt Affie. "Where did she ever get such talent, do you suppose?"

This was too much; Peter began to feel an explosive wrath.

"Look at all *my* pretty pictures," crowed the old lady, bobbing her head toward the grandiose canvases in their gilded frames. "Not really first-rate, are they? Too pretty-pretty. No, no, don't be kind. Rubbish, rubbish, rubbish. Except the Tiepolo in the Green Room. Did you show her the Tiepolo, Eddie?"

"Him, Auntie C., *him*." He shrugged his plump shoulders, spread his hands in defeat. "It's a copy, the Tiepolo. They're all copies. The originals were in the old Abbey."

"Speak up, Eddie! Does she want to copy the Tiepolo?"

"No, no. I was telling him the Ti—"

"Yes! Tea! Where's our tea?" Her head, still cocked to one side, swiveled toward the door. "Where is Eldred? I want my tea, I want my tea."

Edward pulled a bell rope beside the fireplace; the man in black came in like a shadow. "Hadleigh, where's my brother, d'you know?"

"Dr. El just came down, sir. He's changing."

"That's too much to hope for, I'm afraid. But jog him along, Hadleigh. We're ready for tea."

"Look! Look!" Miss Celestia was making fluttery signs toward the window. Peter saw nothing.

"Oh, you missed them, you missed them. You didn't look quick enough."

"What was it, dear?" murmured Aunt Affie.

"Two angels!"

Edward drew in his chin. "Surely not *two*, Auntie C."

"Two of them, wing to wing!"

Aunt Affie bustled to the window and peered out. "Oh, shoot. Wish I'd seen 'em."

"You've got to look fast," wheezed the old lady. "They zip right along. God's messengers don't ride horses, you know."

Before the silence following this piece of news could be broken, the door opened and a man who could only have been Edward's brother joined them. The same cold, brilliant eyes and slippery lips, the same pattern of baldness, only Dr. El was slimmer and more energetic, with a nervous habit of palm-brushing his scanty hair.

Peter, shaking hands with him, was repelled by the spitty gleam of his gums, exposed in an unctuous smile.

"Tea!" Miss Celestia banged her fist on the arm of the wheelchair.

It was a demand, not an announcement, yet the word was no sooner out than the genie Hadleigh arrived, pushing a cart heaped with silver and goodies.

"Ah . . ." Miss Celestia wiggled her fingers like an arthritic at the keyboard.

Edward did the honors, however; Miss Celestia looked hardly strong enough to lift the tiny cup to her lips. Dr. El quizzed Peter on his interests, schoolwork, family, friends, appearing to find each dull response equally fascinating.

As Peter answered these questions to which someone less trusting than he might have suspected the doctor already knew the answers, he gradually became aware that something funny was happening to Miss Celestia.

Each time he glanced at her, he surprised in her eyes what might have been a mocking confidence, as if silently, or in so low a whisper the others couldn't hear it, she were asking him questions of her own.

At first he paid no attention, thought it was his imagination. But no, there it came again, that same look, a visibly guarded narrowing of observation, as rational as it was intense.

As soon as Dr. El had squeezed him dry of information and he was happily ignored, he tried experimentally to answer those secret flashes with signals of his own, and as he did so became certain that he and the old lady were establishing a mysterious, private rapport.

He couldn't guess what it meant, if anything. Consequently, when tea was almost finished, he was excited when she said abruptly, "Rest of you all stay here. I want to show her my Tiepolo. Come, my pet, you may wheel me to the Green Room. Gangway there!"

Edward blocked Peter's move toward the chair.

"Now, now, Auntie C. You know you always rest after tea."

"Don't want to rest!" Once more Peter felt the signals darting from her eyes, faster now, urgent messages. "I want to show her my Tiepolo!"

Her eyes seemed to expand, throb, burn with the urgency of their cryptic message, so urgent she seemed unwilling to waste time codifying it, until, spent with the effort of so naked and mute an appeal, she slumped in the chair, her cranky expression fading into vagueness.

"I'll call Weems." Dr. El reached for the bell rope.

"We've tuckered her out, poor soul," said Aunt Affie, although Peter could have sworn the mood among the brothers and Aunt Affie was one of relaxing tension.

Something touched him: not terror; not even fear, unless it was the sort of fear one has of a neighbor whose ways are mysterious and private and whose windows are always curtained, creating a legend of evil which neither logic nor daylight can ever quite argue away.

In came a woman of statuesque ugliness: dead eyes in a red face and a nose like a peeled shrimp.

"Ah, Weems," said Edward. "Will you take Miss Celestia up, please. Our prattle has tired her."

Wordlessly, the woman stooped and secured Miss Celestia's feet on the footrests and tucked in the afghan.

The old lady momentarily roused herself, looked straight at Peter, and said in a thin, shrill voice, "Don't forget—*Lucifer* was an angel!"

Weems whisked her away.

"Only one word for her," said Edward piously. "Indomitable."

Peter wasn't sure if he meant Miss Celestia or Weems.

Dr. El then suggested Peter might wish to see the secret

room, but as soon as they were outside the Long Gallery he whispered, "Perhaps a brief detour to the lavatory first?"

Repelled by his sticky tone, Peter said no, he didn't have to go. Dr. El smiled, salmon-gummed, avuncular. "Don't have to wee-wee?"

Peter insisted he did not.

"It's just that I was watching you in there. Of course, she's enough to make anyone squirm, poor thing."

"She's awfully old, isn't she?"

"So old she's ageless. Like the Sphinx."

In the hall he showed Peter a certain banister in the staircase. "Grasp it firmly and give it a full twist counter-clockwise."

A faint rumbling sound and a section of the paneled wall beneath the staircase slid back. Stooping, Dr. El led him into a small, square room, bare and airless, where they had to stand hunchbacked. Peter remarked on the lack of ventilation.

"You must remember," said Dr. El, "it's only a replica of the original room in the English house."

As he was about to lead Peter back toward the Long Gallery, Peter touched his arm.

"Where is Welcome?"

As he'd hoped, Dr. El was taken by surprise.

"I know why she's here," Peter added.

Dr. El smiled. "Then one ought to congratulate you on a metaphysical breakthrough. *I've* never discovered why any of us is here."

"I wasn't speaking philosophically." He felt more at ease with Dr. El than with Edward, and he wasn't at all intimidated by him.

"I fear it's the *only* way I can speak. Be it about a mine disaster or a broken shoelace."

Even to the touch, he would be slippery as a fish, thought Peter. It was rather fun to bait him.

"Don't your patients sometimes need more than philosophy?"

Dr. El palm-brushed his hair. "Oh, my practice is one thing; my preaching's quite another."

"Why won't you tell me about Welcome?"

"Professional ethics, dear boy."

"I just want to help her."

Dr. El struck a pose, lips pursed, chin trapped between

26

thumb and forefinger; the caricature of a waggish schoolmaster about to have the fun of birching a saucy pupil. "Laudable, dear boy; however, there are others eminently better qualified. But come, you haven't seen the library."

Motes of dust drifted on slanted sunbeams; the house was tomb-quiet. Peter sensed that Dr. El was trying to divert his attention from something happening elsewhere in the house: an air of deadly seriousness lay like an ill-hidden corpse behind his dreamy eyes and frivolous manner.

Saying nothing, Peter allowed Dr. El to show him the library, by far the pleasantest room, perhaps because the books at least were real and looked as if they'd been handled by real people, instead of being museum replicas.

"This was always Auntie C.'s favorite haunt." From his tone she might have been dead. "She was an avid reader."

"So am I," said Peter.

"I was myself at your age. Alas, no more. In youth, one believes everything one reads. Later, one reads only what one believes. Either way, it's quite useless. The lesson is soon learned. The only difference between Life and Art is that one is a shadow, the other a rainbow. Both are illusions."

For a moment Dr. El's face reminded Peter of Daddy's after a hard day downtown, totally vulnerable, and he took advantage of this to ask again about Welcome. "I'd like to say good-bye to her, if I may."

"I shall do it for you," Dr. El replied.

"Couldn't I just—"

"She's resting, dear boy. Now why the long face? You look like an El Greco cherub. And that's wrong, you know. You're pure Rubens. Tell me the truth, now: have you got a crush on the young woman?"

"I just want to be sure she's okay."

"But how droll. I assure you, she is, and will remain so. She'll always be as carefree as a sunbeam. Will you, cherub? Regrettably, no. Neither you nor I. The obedience that makes *us* free is limited to a few rose-red childish days. No, please don't look at me like that. To stare at sinking ships is an insult to the unrescuable. Come with me. No! Wait here. Don't go away."

He pinched Peter's arm as if stapling him to the spot, a pose Peter held till he was out of sight, and then, grimly assessing the situation, pondered an assault on the upper regions where she must be held. One glance of the valentine face was all he wanted, to be sure she was really all right.

Through the window a glimpse of garden paths, formal as Mondrian mindscapes. Flower beds, trellises, fountains beneath storybook clouds in an aqueous sky. His fantasies vanished. All indeed rainbows and shadows and no more mysterious than a sunny day at the circus. Buy your ticket at the main gate. Enchanted Garden? To your left beyond the myrtle tree, sir. The Mad Doctor? The Secret Chamber? To your right, madame, and up the stairs.

But now Dr. El was back, shoving a framed photograph into his hand: a man's face, doe-eyed, rose-lipped, hair a sea of highlights and shadows.

"Before the storm."

"Storm?"

"Of life. 'Bare ruined choirs where late the sweet birds sang.' "

Peter studied the picture as if it were of someone neither of them knew, as indeed it was. He could think of nothing to say. Finally Dr. El sighed, took it from him, and held it before his own eyes like a mirror; then, with a puckish smile, he looked down at Peter.

"Before we rejoin the others, perhaps you'd now like to stop off at the lavatory?"

His smile paled into wistfulness as Peter, who did want to but wouldn't admit it, refused.

As they were all saying good-bye, Aunt Affie asked him the same question, whispering in his ear. He was inspired to try something rash.

He excused himself and headed for the stairs, taking Dr. El by surprise and imperiously waving him back when he offered to show him the way.

"I'll find it!" he cried, running across the hall and up the stairs.

He heard Aunt Affie's chuckle. "Land sakes, I guess he *did* have to go!"

The stupidity of this act was apparent the moment he crossed the gallery out of their sight, for instead of one central hall he was faced by a warren of narrow passageways branching off into the various wings. He opened a couple of doors at random. The passage he'd chosen suddenly jogged, went up two steps, and divided into two more passages. It was quite hopeless. Had he dared, he would have called her name.

He came to a narrow staircase and decided he might as well go back down. It led into an enormous kitchen or scullery, where a skinny girl in a white smock looked at him without surprise and, with a smile, went back to the pot she was scouring.

Seconds later he found himself behind a half-open door leading into the hall. He stopped short. Aunt Affie and Edward Breed were almost close enough to touch. Dr. El was just going up the main staircase.

"He'll come around," Peter heard Edward say as soon as Dr. El was out of sight. "As soon as he's found a way to satisfy his own peculiar sense of decorum."

"I don't understand." She sounded peevish.

"Simply that he's the sort of man for whom motives of expedience reek of vulgarity. He must always pretty them up. Find something philosophical or artistic to redeem them."

"And *I* thought it was a simple question of survival."

"So it is, my dear Mrs. Juul. But he distrusts anything simple." Peter saw him crane his neck toward the gallery. "I hope he doesn't scare the brat."

"Does your brother have to approve?"

"If we're to have his help, yes."

"And you still think he will?"

"Oh, decidedly."

"He's done wonders with her."

"A genius in his way. I suppose one must tolerate his whims."

"But is there time?"

"Time?"

"It's got to be done soon."

"He's quite aware of that."

"I wish to goodness it was over and done with. I shan't get a good night's sleep till it is."

Edward laughed. "Better have him give you something."

"Not on your life!"

At this, they both chuckled.

Peter didn't dare wait any longer. Dr. El might find him there. He stepped noisily into the hall behind them, pleased by Aunt Affie's little yip of surprise.

"Lost my way," he said innocently.

"Dr. El's looking for you," she said crossly. "Come along now. Krieg's a'waitin'. I don't fancy drivin' in the dark."

He felt better as soon as he saw Krieg.

All the way home no one said a word about Welcome. Krieg was silent behind the wheel, and Aunt Affie's complaints of weariness bore traces of some vague displeasure.

Clouds reshape the landscape; thus Peter saw nothing familiar about the road that next morning until they were passing the very spot where he and Krieg had stopped and taken refreshment, each in his own way, on the trip from Plato Switch to Brokenstraw. Involuntarily, he cried out. Krieg said nothing, but Aunt Affie pinched his arm.

"Sure enough is the Plato Switch Road, darlin'. Only we turn off it in a little bit."

They soon did, along another dirt road hacked through rocky hills thick with laurel and sassafras, until they came to a sign at the foot of a narrow, uphill lane:

SUGAR HILL FARM. THERON JUUL.

Peter would later write in his diary: "Picture wind waves of grass around an islandlike knoll, a brick house streakily faded to a rusty pink, with a cupola spiked with lightning rods and a porch and high narrow windows painted mustard-yellow."

Aunt Affie had raved about her two grandchildren with such fulsome pride that Peter was ready to hate them on sight. His first glimpse, however, was of their father, a big, loose-knit man, not fat but with an abundance of flesh, as if nature, having had too much material to work with, had stretched it out wherever possible, leaving too wide a gap between the eyes, between lip and nose, brow and hairline, shoulder and waist: a lack of compactness that was almost sloppy. His hair was coarse and gingery and his skin the color of burnt oatmeal. He was dressed like a farmer, although Peter didn't see a speck of dust on his polished leather boots.

His jovial, witless remarks about "our little city cousin" convinced Peter that Theron Juul would never do or say anything of the slightest interest. He was no Krieg.

Aunt Affie dropped into one of the wicker porch chairs and looked off at the cool blue line of the Brokenstraw Ridge. The wind shifted, bringing to Peter's nose the earthy tang of horse manure, and he looked around at the silos and barns and outbuildings behind the house, at fields of corn and buckwheat and hay, at cows and more cows, and at the impervious pines beyond. Starlings shrilled over the waves of grass like gulls over water. He had never felt so isolated, nor so far from home.

Theron slouched to the door in his squeaky boots and bellowed, "Cleo! They're here!"

The yellow door opened and Cleo Juul came out to greet them, a tall, sallow woman with a mass of black hair parted to frame her face in a dark triangle; thin pink lips, a longish but elegant nose, and curiously radiant eyes that saved her face from plainness.

Peter stared at that face with stunned disbelief.

It was the face of the dark lady he'd seen lying naked in Krieg's arms.

Part Two

He hated the farm and he hated her.

From the beginning the farm was the lengthened shadow of this dark lady, this "languid villainess" as he described her in his diary, who was the exact opposite of Welcome, her face not a valentine but a Greek mask that revealed no hint of those passionate emotions for which he despised her.

Perhaps any attempt to interest him in the farm would have failed anyway, for he hadn't the right temperament; exposure to the country had come too late to engage his sympathies. There was no enchantment to be found in woods and farmyard for an imagination nurtured by an urban mystique and reared on a diet of Stevenson and Conan Doyle. He had woven his dreams behind city windows, with always the dull roar of traffic in the background.

In short, he would have been totally bored if he hadn't been frightened.

When he asked himself what he was frightened *of*, he could offer only the vaguest answer, and it was in fact the vagueness of his fear, its elusiveness, that caused him the most anxiety.

Though no one had done or said anything to threaten him, he felt menaced by something as pervasive as it was irrational; it was like hearing the footsteps of a pursuer who was never there when you turned around, like the hovering phantom of disaster in a bad dream.

And based on what? Nothing more alarming than a pregnant female servant, a farmhand having an affair with his boss's wife, and a few stray fragments of conversation which at worst were no more than ambiguous.

The feeling that in some mysterious way he was affected by these things troubled him, put him on edge, and even made him distrust the way everyone treated him. They were unnaturally polite, they were too kind, they smiled too quickly, asked too often how he was feeling, stopped talking too abruptly when he came into a room. It was the way a hopeless invalid would be treated. To spite them, he played up to the role; moping for hours in his room or on the much cooler veranda, where tinkling wind chimes above the swing added delicate background music to his performance.

He had never been one of those boys who are wild about animals; they pleased him only as figures in a landscape and, rampant or couchant, upon a coat of arms; real ones bored him. He found the Juul children even more boring than animals: Maureen, seventeen, fat, pasty, and snobbish; Luke, two years younger, chubby and slothlike. Both were spoiled, secretive, and touchy, and both ignored Peter, not out of shyness as he'd first thought, but out of some subtler, more furtive hostility.

Hoping to learn more about Welcome, Peter made an effort to be friendly with Luke, an effort hampered by the boy's sullenness and by his perpetual dreary absorption in his guitar, on which he played what he called "real bluegrass stuff," droning out the lyrics in a mournful houndlike tenor.

"Did you know she was going to have a baby?" Peter asked him.

He plucked a sour note from his E string. "Hell, yes."

"What about the father?"

"So what about him?"

"You know who he is?"

"Maybe."

His heavy foot began beating time on the porch step.

"Tell me."

Luke sniffed. "What the hell for?"

"I'm interested."

Luke eyed him briefly. "What'll you give me?"

"Will you tell me?"

"I said, what'll you give me?"

Peter thought about it. "One of my sketches?"

"Forget it."

"I don't have any money."

Luke gave him a sly glance. "Show me your thing and I might."

"My what?"

"Your *thing*, you dope. You know. Your jigger. Dingus. Joy knob."

Peter was genuinely shocked. "Why should I do that?"

"Betcha don't have one. You look like a pansy."

Peter stood up. "You probably don't even know who the father is."

"Like hell I don't. You think I'm as stupid as you? I know all about Welcome and all of them. I—"

Peter looked around. Aunt Affie stood inside the screen door listening to them.

Luke gave him a truly venomous look. "It ain't none o' your business, snoop!" Clutching his guitar, he jumped off the porch and ran down the lane.

Although no one treated him any differently that night at the dinner table, Peter noticed that Theron was very short with Luke, who didn't open his mouth except to shove the food in. As Theron left the table at the end of the meal, he put his hand down hard on Luke's shoulder. "Quick as you're done feedin' your face, you haul your hide upstairs." His tone was ominous.

Peter stayed in his own room until he heard Luke close his father's bedroom door, then he stole down the hall, made sure no one was about, and pressed his ear to the keyhole.

He first heard a loud slap, followed by a whine of pained surprise from Luke, and a peevish, cringing protest.

"What'd you have to go an' do that for?"

"So's you'll know I mean business, Lukey boy."

"You didn't have to hit me."

"That's just a sample what you got comin' you don't watch that fool tongue o' yours."

"I didn't tell the little bastard nothin'."

Peter's eyes were fixed on the top of the stairs, body tensed to spring away from the door if anyone came up.

Theron said, "She heard you, so don't gimme none o' that shit."

"I didn't! Don't hit me—"

"You callin' your granny a liar, boy?"

"Naw! But I ain't lyin' neither. He was tryin' to pump me. I didn't tell him nothin'."

"Shut up!"

"I didn't!"

"We told you to steer clear o' him."

Luke's tone soured. "If the little bastard's so sick, how come he came here, anyway?"

"All you gotta remember is he is sick, an' you stay away from him or you're gonna catch it."

Puzzled interest from Luke. "You mean he's got somethin' catchin'."

"You smart talkin' me, boy?"

"Naw! I—"

"I mean you're gonna catch it from me, Lukey boy. With the mean end of a razor strop, you do any more blabbin'."

Luke started to whine an answer to this when Peter heard footsteps on the stairs. In a flash he was behind his own door, hearing Aunt Affie say, as Luke came into the hall, "You seen Peter, darlin'?"

"Naw! An' I don't wanna!"

Peter heard him clattering downstairs and, a moment later, Aunt Affie's gentle knock on Theron's door.

Peter sat down on the bed, as weak as if he'd fallen there from a great height.

All you gotta remember is he is sick . . .

He pressed his hand to his heart as if to measure the regularity of its beat.

He had been so sure they were all plotting to keep him in the dark about something. Those overheard snatches of conversation, all the guardedness and double-talk: what else could it mean? Naturally, he'd assumed it was something about *them* he wasn't supposed to know. Something about Welcome and Mr. Breed and Miss Celestia.

But maybe not. Maybe it was something about *him!*

That air of sly delicacy with which they all treated him, the things they asked: "How are you feeling today, Peter?" "You're not getting tired, are you, Peter?" "You'd better come in and rest before dinner, Peter, dear." "You look a bit peaked this morning, Peter."

He snatched up a hand mirror and searched his face for some dreadful sign, a yellow pallor, a sunken eye. It might all be a conspiracy—even Mother and Daddy might be in on it! He would have known if they'd sent him to a sanatorium, having read enough about those places, full of wilting invalids sent there to die, doped to the teeth, and laid out in the sun and told not to get tired; no, they wouldn't have dared send him to one of those places, he was too shrewd, he would have guessed. Whereas here . . .

"Home?" Aunt Affie couldn't have looked more like

Gram if she had worn her face. "Why, darlin' boy, you just got here."

"But I don't feel good."

She felt of his head. "That's what you're here for, honey lamb. You got to give it a chance. Where don't you feel good?"

She was lying, covering up.

"I don't know. All over."

"Tell me the honest truth now. You're just sufferin' a twinge of homesickness, ain't that right? Ain't that what's afflictin' you?"

"No!" He hated being treated like an imbecilic baby.

A crispness entered her tone. "Well, then. You know I can't just bundle you home for no good reason at all. Your darlin' mama's dependin' on me to make you all well. I think maybe we better call in Dr. El to have a look at you."

He recoiled from this idea, whereupon she smiled as if she had trapped an elusive animal by attacking its weakest defense. "Dr. El's taken quite a fancy to you. Did you know that?"

She wasn't Gram now; the act was over. "Oh, indeedy he has. He thinks you're one peach of a boy. He'd soon find out what's ailin' you. Dr. El's real thorough when he examines somebody. 'Specially somebody he's taken such a fancy to."

"It's nothing like that. It's—"

"Not scared of Dr. El, are you, darlin'?"

"No."

"He wouldn't hurt you. Dr. El wouldn't hurt a fly. He'd be real gentle with you. But thorough. Maybe you're a little bit bashful. That it? Ain't you never been examined real thorough before?"

He could imagine the gummy simper on Dr. El's face, the delight with which those clammy, womanish hands would poke and prod.

"I'm not that sick. Just don't feel so hot, that's all."

"I understand, darlin'." Her expression was maddening.

He would write to Mother himself. She'd understand. She wouldn't want him to stay where he wasn't happy. Where he was . . . frightened.

"Know what I think you need, darlin'? You've been mopin' around the house too much. Fresh air and exercise. That's what you need."

He could have laughed in her face. What about all her pious injunctions that he must constantly rest, not get overheated?

"I'm goin' to tell Krieg he's got to spend more time with you."

He wrote to Mother that night, meaning to tell her everything, but when it came to reducing it all to words, he was stumped. He could point to nothing concrete. No one had mistreated him; quite the opposite. His sense of unease was too shadowy to explain, and whatever he said, the impression would be left that he was indeed only homesick. In the end, he tore up the letter.

The following day Krieg took upon himself the task of teaching Peter to ride, spending the whole day in the livery stable patiently instructing the boy in the fundamentals of horsemanship, allowing him to do everything but mount a horse, for which Peter was silently grateful. The creatures looked splendid, but he would as enthusiastically have ridden an alligator.

Within a few days, however, he was more familiar with the livery stable than with any other part of the farm. The stableman was called Poley—short for Napoleon—a gaunt, sinewy character of fifty-five or sixty with a cast in his right eye and a jaw that gave him a decidedly horsy look, a coincidence Peter found more sinister than amusing. He'd been at his shyest around this "leering centaur," as he described him in his diary, until, after several visits, Poley allowed him to brush and curry and comb the horses, a practice that helped him overcome his shyness of the animals as well.

After this it was not surprising that Peter, who had often enough played at being a knight in armor on a two-wheeled bike, took to this new pastime with freshness and delight, especially when Krieg declared that he showed a natural aptitude for the sport.

Krieg chose Peter's mount, but it was Poley who told him that Cleo had previously ridden the same horse every day, until the week before Peter arrived, when the horse had thrown her. She hadn't been on him since. When Peter mentioned this to Krieg later, the older man seemed displeased that Poley had talked about it.

"Why did he throw her?" Peter asked. "Did something spook him?"

Krieg grinned. "His rider."

"Cleo?"

Krieg didn't answer. Peter watched him closely.

"Were you with her when it happened?"

"Yes."

"Did you always go riding with her?"

"Not always." Krieg's face was clear of thought, as absently amused as it always looked; certainly there was no hint of a guilty conscience.

Peter was annoyed. He would have given anything to let Krieg know that he knew all about him and Cleo. He had tried to spy on them without giving the game away, but they were too cautious.

There were too many places they could slip away to and not be found, acres of woods and fields. "Between the acres of the rye these pretty country folk would lie." The memory of what he'd seen in the glade stirred a fresh wave of jealousy.

He couldn't ask Krieg about Cleo—he hadn't quite the nerve for that—but one day he felt brave enough to tackle the subject of Mr. Breed and Welcome. They had ridden to one of Peter's favorite spots, a woodland pool about three miles from the farm. There was a makeshift diving board and a tiny dory. The day was unusually hot, and they had lost no time in tying the horses to a tree, stripping off their clothes, and jumping into the chilly water.

While they were splashing around, Peter said, "Krieg, tell me something. Do you like Mr. Breed?"

"He's okay, I guess."

"He didn't like me."

"He say so?"

"Not to my face. After I'd left the room."

"Then how'd you know?"

"Snuck back and listened. He said I was sly."

"Kid who sneaks around listening at keyholes?" Krieg was seldom ironic; when he was, it had a nice manly bite to it.

"What's wrong with being curious?"

Krieg splashed him in the face. "About stuff that ain't none of your business?"

Peter looked innocent. "I suppose it's none of my business what he said about Welcome, either. Or you."

He thrust himself backward, thrashed the water with his

hands, but all Krieg did was laugh and say, "Sport, somethin' tells me you're gonna be a smart-ass troublemaker."

"*I* didn't make the trouble Welcome's in." He was afraid he'd gone too far, seriously offended Krieg.

"She in trouble?" Krieg pulled himself up out of the pool and shook his head dog-fashion and dropped down on the crackly sun-warmed grass. Peter followed him.

"I'm not blind, you know. Welcome's going to have a baby, and she isn't even married."

"Kid your age ain't supposed to think about such things."

"I'm not an infant. You're as bad as Aunt Affie. You'd be surprised what I think about."

"God Almighty, sport, you tryin' to tell me *you're* to blame for Welcome's baby?"

Peter quickly strangled a shrill, explosive laugh. "I never even *knew* her till I came here!"

Krieg shrugged.

"Besides . . ."

"What?"

"Nothing."

"Spit it out."

"Well, it so happens I'm a v-i-r-g-i-n, in case you're wondering." His nerve astonished him.

Krieg squinted at him. "Hell you are."

"Don't you believe me?" Until now it had been only in bed at night, in the privacy of his own mind, that he had ever talked like this.

Krieg wasn't treating it as anything exceptional; his very composure, that tough, unruffled smile, added to Peter's enjoyment.

"You say so, sure."

"Then tell me the truth, Krieg—" too late to back off— "Is the baby—are you—did you—"

"Knock her up?"

The roughness of the expression delighted Peter. "Well . . ."

"You're gettin' awful damn personal, sport."

"Then you don't deny it."

"Believe me if I did?"

"Sure."

"Tell you one thing, sport. I ain't no v-i-r-g-i-n."

"If you're to blame and don't marry her, you're a swine."

39

His tone had been only mildly abusive, but still he cringed. Again, Krieg responded with only a lazy, absent-minded smile.

"Maybe I ain't the marryin' kind, sport."

"I don't understand you."

"Forget it, sport."

I should despise him, Peter thought. To be so callous. Maybe he didn't really care. Maybe Cleo had made him forget all about Welcome. But he didn't despise him. He admired him more than ever, somehow, wished passionately he could be like him, look as rough and tough, swear as casually, and more than anything else, be as *unmoved* by everything.

"Am I getting tan yet?" he said shyly.

Krieg looked at him. "A bit, I think. Give it time, sport."

Peter knew he was lying, but he didn't care; by summer's end he'd be a luscious dark honey color like Krieg—and suddenly he thought of the letter to Mother and was glad he hadn't mailed it because he didn't honestly want to go home, not now that he and Krieg were having so much fun together, not when he had a real friend at last.

As his glance moved along Krieg's side, he discovered something very strange.

Krieg had a scar on his thigh just below the groin, the oddest scar Peter had ever seen: pale, wizened tissue formed an almost perfect five-pointed star about the size of a dime.

"Where'd you get that, Krieg?"

"What? Oh, that. Birthmark."

"Shaped like a star?"

"Jesus, you're a nosy little bastard."

Peter was pleased to have got even this meager rise out of him. "Sorry I asked."

"Then wipe that smirk off your face." Krieg rolled over onto his belly, water beads sliding off his back, muscles softening.

Peter glanced down at himself, thinking how no dark lady or light lady or any other kind of lady would want to lie with him, and he wondered if he would ever be, could ever be, like Krieg; there seemed such a vast, essential difference between them.

But such reflections were part of an abiding mystery too private even for the secret pages of his diary. When he made that day's entry, all he mentioned was the star on Krieg's thigh.

As an afterthought, he added: *I don't think it's a birthmark.*

He soon made a more curious discovery.

From his bedroom window he could look down at the stable, and one night, awakened by the sound of horses hooves, he got up just in time to see Cleo—it had to be Cleo with that long black hair—riding off in the moonlight toward the woods.

On her way to a midnight tryst with Krieg? Was this the pattern of their affair?

The thought troubled him, made him angry and jealous, for he felt that Krieg had deceived him; besides, it was so unfair to Welcome.

No good going back to bed; he had to know. It would be simple to slip down to the stable and see if Krieg's horse was also missing.

Everything looks mysteriously larger at night: the sun has a way of shrinking things, while the moon stretches and expands the visible; and it was with a shivery feeling of exploring the unknown that he made his way across the farmyard.

At the stable door, as he was lifting the heavy latch, an odd thing happened.

A faint cry, directionless as an echo, hung for a moment in the still night air.

Fear came in its wake, twisting the shadows into shapes of menace.

He first thought Cleo might have been thrown, but then it came again, louder this time, apparently from the barn, and unmistakably human.

When he got to the barn and looked back at the house, dark and silent upon the grassy knoll, for a moment fear nearly outweighed the curiosity that had drawn him this far. He paused. The cry was repeated, and something stronger than merely innocent curiosity urged him to investigate its source.

Opening a small side door, he stepped into the barn. Tractors and other pieces of machinery were stored at this end of the structure, and he threaded his way among them to a middle area lined with wooden grain bins. A single bulb created a confusion of shadows but helped him pick his way between the rows of bins, his slippered feet noiseless on the concrete floor. Once he nearly tripped on a sluiceway.

Once more he heard the cry, loud and tremulous, and again the urge to retreat from what he suspected was a mystery he might not be ready to cope with was almost strong enough to send him running from the barn back to his own cozy, familiar room. As it was, he waited a good two minutes pressed hard against the whitewashed wall, before peering around the corner.

A red bulb glowed above the spot where prize steers were ordinarily tethered to be groomed, ropes from either wall holding them immobile in the middle of the areaway. Only now it was not a steer hooked to those ropes; it was a man, a naked, hairy brute whom Peter had often seen cleaning out the stalls in the stable, a dim-witted slobbering creature, repulsive as a gargoyle.

One of the dairymaids, a buxom, jolly girl who had often smiled so modestly at Peter from the milkhouse window, stood naked and booted behind the bound man, wielding a horsewhip with savage zest.

The whole scene was bathed in the crimson light of that one dim bulb, giving it all an even more hellish aspect, so that Peter did not immediately make out the other person present, sitting stiffly on a bale of straw a few feet away, his legs spread apart, his head bent forward.

It was Theron Juul, and Peter saw enough of the pumping motion of his arm to know what he was doing and to be aghast at the sight.

"You look peaked, darlin'," observed Aunt Affie, so sugar-tongued that the cry of murder would have sounded like the sweetest endearment.

"It was hot last night. I couldn't sleep."

"You be sure you take a nap this afternoon."

As if a nap could blot out that scene!

"Going riding with Krieg," he answered dully.

"Too hot for that. You'll be sick; see if you're not."

They rode only as far as the pond, where he stripped and slid into the water, content to float on his back, eyes fixed on a blue sky scantily feathered with quill-shaped clouds, and to dream of being up there in those airy acres of emptiness instead of down here where nature's face screened mysteries as cruel and sensual as did the barn's whitewashed walls: worlds in torment, lust and death among the insects, botanical parasites, rapacious birds, cancerous fungi, rot and decay everywhere.

And, oh, the unthinkable mindless *jolliness* of Krieg in the face of such horrors! He and Welcome were so alike in that respect, seemingly insensible to the brutal forces at work around and upon them. Look at him lounging on the bank, that handsome, happy face, so sure of itself, so smug; that strong, nude body, so armored with muscle and sun its very nudity was a shield, revealing nothing of the man inside.

He hadn't meant to tell Krieg, and yet he wanted very much to torment him, to shatter his infuriating composure, to *move* him; and this seemed perhaps a way of doing it.

But the tale he told of what he'd seen aroused not even a shadow of concern on Krieg's bland, passive face.

"But he might be dead!" cried Peter.

"Then why didn't you do something about it?"

"I was scared."

"Guess maybe you knew they wasn't really hurtin' him." Krieg lazily nibbled a blade of grass.

Peter stared at him in rage.

"Not *hurt*ing—they were murdering him!"

Krieg only laughed. "Ease off, sport. Ain't nobody been murdered."

"How do you know?"

"I just know."

"You weren't even there. I know where *you* were."

He was glad it slipped out.

"Oh? Where?"

Peter looked at him. "With her."

"Who the hell's her?"

"Cleo!"

He was prepared to dodge a blow, but again all he got was a smile of casual indifference; Krieg's thoughts might have been a million miles away.

"That's why I woke up. I heard her. And I saw her riding off into the woods."

Krieg reached out and cupped Peter's jaw in his big palm.

"Sport, when you gonna learn to keep your nose outa other folks' business?"

Peter jerked his head away. "What is it you're all afraid I'll find out?"

"You just don't know country folks, sport."

Peter decided it was time to get nasty.

"If I tell Aunt Affie—"

"You won't."

"If I do—"

"You won't if you know what's good for you."

"But that poor guy—"

Krieg sprang lightly to his feet. "Get your duds on, sport. There's something you better see."

"Locky? He aroun' here somewheres." Poley's grin widened, displaying horse-pink gums.

"Well, where?" Krieg's voice had an unaccustomed snap.

Weathered lids tightened across Poley's eyes. "Oh, wal, Locky, he ain't feelin' too chipper right now."

"Where is he?"

Peter saw the look that passed between Poley and Krieg. Krieg gave a short nod. Poley shrugged, looked uncertainly from Krieg to Peter, then jerked his thumb toward the end of the stable, shambling after them as Krieg led the way.

In one of the empty stalls, lying on a horse blanket over a heap of straw, the man Peter had watched being whipped dozed in a fog of liquor and liniment, two empty bottles beside him and a third, half-full of whisky, close by his hand. A gooey salve made his body gleam where raw welts crisscrossed his muscled torso.

With needless cruelty, Peter thought, Krieg prodded the man awake with his booted toe. Locky stirred, groaned more in drunkenness than in pain, then, at another prod, came more fully awake, looking up at them with bleary animal eyes—horse eyes, thought Peter—and then a sort of idiot comprehension broke over his face, splitting it into a fatuous grin. A bubble of spit formed beside his mouth, and he raised a fist to wipe it away, streaking his stubbled chin.

"What the hell happened to you, Locky?" asked Krieg with a laugh.

Locky made gobbling noises. Poley smiled. "This crazy ole fool Locky, he cleanin' out Pal-O-Mine's stall yestiddy an' he let hisself git jammed agin that wall an' git all scraped up."

Krieg looked at Peter with an innocently sociable smile.

"Locky here's always getting banged up. I think he likes it. Ain't that so, Locky?"

At this Locky made a deep, satisfied, chortling sound, rolled his eyes and nodded, breathing heavily and seeming to Peter to take immense delight in this attention, then suddenly throwing off the blanket before Poley could stop him and, like a soldier displaying his battle wounds, pointing out old lines of scar tissue ringing his leathery brown body.

Peter felt sick.

"Country capers, sport," said Krieg later, dismissing it all with an idle shrug. "They get pretty rough sometimes."

Peter stared at him as if he were speaking a foreign tongue.

"Locky likes bein' whupped. And Rebecca likes doin' it. And Mr. Juul"—Peter detected a sliver of contempt—"well, he gets a kick out of watchin'. So don't get all cranked up about it, okay?"

Peter was silent, reflecting upon something beyond this, something far more singular than Locky's welts and scars and his outlandish demented pride in them.

It was what he'd seen on Locky's groin before Poley had quickly covered it with a blanket:

A star, pale and wizened, identical to Krieg's.

The Aspern Papers was ordinarily a dependable means of escape, yet now its magic failed to work; his imagination seemed dead, and when he came to that unfortunate phrase, "I had not meant by my private ejaculation ..." he was forced to give up the effort, fling the book aside, and let the world crash down upon him with all its jarring aggravations. The sun mocked him with its ageless, idiot stare. It was all so senseless and boring, *this* world where, as he wrote in his diary that night, "people don't merely suffer pain—they revel in it."

A significant entry, as it turned out.

In the sticky heat of the afternoon, when his breath seemed drawn through layers of flannel, he held a mirror in one hand and studied his face in the oval glass, turning to let the sun fall across his left cheek, making his face more interesting, giving it depth and character, creating something dramatic of the shallow cleft in his chin ... Suddenly he thought of something to add to last night's entry in his diary, and he sprang up to get it from the bureau drawer.

It was gone.

Neither was his return ticket there.

Stricken, he raised his eyes to the window and saw the far-off gateless wall of the Brokenstraw Ridge, and the sky above, terrible in its emptiness. His gaze traveled to the mirror, still lying face up on the bed, a sphere of blankness, a silent zero....

The house itself was absolutely still, as if everyone in it were listening ... listening ...

"You're not eating, darlin'," said Aunt Affie.

"Yes I am." He forced the spoon to his mouth.

"Not like you have been. Is he, Cleo?"

Cleo's eyes rested unseeingly on his face. "I hadn't noticed, Ma."

Theron reached over and put a hamlike paw on his forehead. "Whew!" He snatched it away. "Kid's burnin' up."

"Been actin' queer all day," said Aunt Affie. "Honey of a day like this, and he ain't been out of the house once."

Their eyes frightened him. "There's nothing wrong with me!"

"Now, darlin', ain't no disgrace to be sick."

"I'm *not* sick."

"Just the same, we ain't takin' no chances. It's up to bed with you the minute you've done eatin'. I'd never forgive myself if somethin' happened to you while you're under my care. How would I ever face your darlin' mama?"

Mother's name pushed him close to tears. "I guess maybe it's time I went home."

No one said a word. They merely kept looking at him, and then Aunt Affie smiled. "Oh, now, I'm sure it ain't nothin' so serious you should spoil your nice vacation and get your folks all riled up. I've got a better idea. We'll have Dr. El come over and have a look at you."

"But there's nothing wrong with me!"

"Then just to humor me, old fussbudget that I am."

"He'll only be wasting his time."

"Dr. El's got all the time in the world. An' like I said, darlin', he sure does love to examine folks."

The thought made him squirm. "He's not going to like it when he finds out you've called him way out here on a wild-goose chase."

On the contrary, Dr. El behaved as if they had done him an extraordinary favor by allowing him to call. He smiled constantly and hummed the *Valse Triste* as he listened to Peter's lungs and heart, and when he tucked his stethoscope back in a bead-embroidered medical bag, he winked at Peter with droll flirtatiousness.

"We'll give you a better going-over later, cherub, but I should say that your aunt's diagnosis was quite accurate, by and large. Too much friskiness. Far too much rambling about."

He paused as if deliberating a choice of remedies, none of which would be in the least disagreeable.

"Yes, I should prescribe a change of scene." His voice dropped, even though they were alone. "How would you fancy a few days at the Abbey, cherub?"

The farm had grown oppressive, but the prospect of Dr. El's company, even at the Abbey, was not enlivening.

Dr. El stroked his fine, whiskerless chin. "I know someone who'd be delighted to see you again."

Peter sniffed the bait warily. "Who?"

"A pretty young damsel of your acquaintance. Your *fond* acquaintance, need I add?"

When Peter still hesitated, he leaned closer. "Besides, wouldn't you rather visit the Abbey than be shut up in this stuffy room for a week—or more?"

Peter spied a subtle threat behind the coaxing tone. He said he would think about it. Dr. El went downstairs to propose the idea to Aunt Affie, for all the world as if they hadn't already cooked it up between them. And for what possible reason other than his having got too close to the truth. How reckless he had been to write everything in his diary.

Dr. El was soon back with Aunt Affie in tow, both of them beaming.

"Peter, darlin', I swear you look better already. You positive he won't be in the way, Dr. El?"

"Perish the thought, dear lady."

"His manners are princely—when he remembers 'em."

Dr. El gave him a secret wink. "A peach of a lad."

Aunt Affie sat down on the bed so heavily that Peter lurched against her. "You don't seem very excited, darlin'," she gushed.

"I'm not supposed to get excited," he replied dryly. "Remember?"

She watched him with a troubled smile, glanced dubiously at Dr. El, then with a more positive expression said briskly, "But you will go, won't you, darlin'?"

Do I have a choice, he felt like asking.

Had Dr. El's face been made of wax, his smile would surely have melted it.

"Then why delay? Unless you've any objections, my dear Mrs. Juul, why not pack his little bag and we can be off at once."

Mrs. Juul had no objections.

During those first few days at the Abbey, he was left more or less to himself, and, as the weather continued to be warm and sunny, he spent most of the time exploring the park and gardens, enjoying a freedom of movement he soon learned was no more than that of a dog's on a leash.

Having ventured one morning to the furthest limits of the park, he was suddenly challenged by a man with a vicious-looking German shepherd, and though the man spoke courteously enough he made it clear to Peter that it would be unwise to stray so far from the Abbey. Likewise, the pleasures of the gardens with their enchanting pergolas, groves, and mazes became less enjoyable when he discovered his every move was watched by one of the numerous gardeners.

Because of this, he began spending more time in the library in a state of nervous anticipation. He knew they had brought him here for a purpose, yet now he was being ignored as earnestly as he had been fussed over at the farm.

There had been no sign of Welcome, and Miss Celestia, he was told, had been confined to her suite for several days with a bad cold.

Peter asked no questions, betrayed no overt curiosity. He might be the mouse in this game, but he would act like the cat.

And then strange things began to happen.

One morning he opened his bureau drawer and was amazed to find his diary lying there in plain sight.

He stared at it for several seconds with the oddest feeling of horror, as if it couldn't really be his diary at all, but something else cleverly disguised as the diary—a bomb, perhaps. When he did at last pick it up, it took a certain amount of courage to leaf through it, as if he were afraid of finding the margins scrawled with threatening or obscene comments.

Then he remembered his return ticket and hastily searched all the drawers to see if that, too, might have been returned.

It hadn't.

At dinner that evening, there was a very puzzling conversation.

Edward was amused by Peter's uneasy glances at one of the family portraits in the dining room, that of a crusty old man whose churlish gaze appeared fixed upon Peter's face whenever he looked up from his plate. Edward assured him the man had been quite as formidable as he looked. Peter asked if he was the Breed who had built the Abbey.

"Re-created it, to be precise." And then, with a hectoring look at his brother, "The Valley owes everything to Azariah Breed. Right, brother El?"

Dr. El agreed, ignoring his brother's mildly bullying tone, and whether it was the doctor's submissiveness that irked Peter or an urge to defy Azariah Breed's haughty glare, he wasn't sure; but something gave him the nerve to say that *he* thought the old man looked more like a monster than a messiah.

This brought a gleeful yelp from Dr. El. Edward wasn't amused.

"His motivations were political," he said stiffly. "There's always an element of the monstrous in politics."

"And seldom any morality," declared his brother.

"I believe it was Vladimir Lenin," retorted Edward icily, "who said there is no morality in politics, only expediency. If you wish to be painted with *that* brush."

Peter asked them if Azariah Breed was in the government.

"My dear boy, he *was* the government. This side of Brokenstraw Ridge." Edward obviously regarded his ancestor with a disciple's esteem.

Dr. El, reflecting upon the portrait with his light, impertinent smile, was less pious. "Can't you just hear him bellowing from the beyond, 'And I still am!' "

"He needn't bellow," snapped Edward. "He has spoken and he has been heard."

"Rubbish, Eddie."

Peter guessed that Dr. El was more or less showing off

49

for his benefit, that alone with his brother he would be less irreverent.

Wine, for which Edward had shown no distaste during the course of the meal, seemed to bring out the stuffy side of his personality. Saluting the portrait with his glass, he said ringingly, "It was his *will!*"

The emphasis on the last word suggested a pun. Peter was intrigued.

"Really, my dear Edward," gibed Dr. El, "you're becoming as pompous as *he* looks. All this talk of wills and spirits. Are we to understand there's been some sort of astral communication? Perhaps even a transmigration? Look at him, cherub. See that *uncanny* resemblance?"

Edward glowered. "Say what you wish. It's all in the journals."

"A matter of interpretation, brother dear. Examine the roots of Christianity, and you'll find a band of hopheads who worshiped mushrooms! Think what a few mythomaniacs with an ignorance of semantics made of *that*."

He appealed to Peter for support.

"I'm afraid I don't know what you're talking about," Peter admitted, embarrassed by Dr. El's theatrical manner.

"Nor does he," said Edward.

"Let us appeal to the wisdom of innocence," said Dr. El coolly. "The situation is this, cherub. Our—"

"Eldred!"

"Oh, be quiet, Eddie. I may raise a ghost or two, but I shan't rattle any skeletons. Now, then. Our illustrious ancestor, whose trenchant gaze understandably unnerves you, cherub, was a ruthless but effective politician. The morality of his politics is neither here nor there."

"Eldred, I protest!"

Dr. El ignored him. "Now, cherub, you be the judge. Azariah Breed was a pragmatist, above and beyond anything else. Landing on this continent with the shreds of his family's fortune, he resorted to certain practices with a view to restoring that fortune as speedily as possible—practices which were, shall we say, ideologically repugnant to his neighbors on the other side of the Ridge. He prospered, as did his relatives, under his direction. Perhaps you aren't aware, my dear cherub, of what a homogeneous community we are. Every family hereabouts is an offshoot, in one way or another, of the Breed line. All of them are blood relatives. In fact, the only branch of the family not living in this valley is represented by—you, cherub."

"Eldred!" Edward was on his feet.

"Sit *down*, Eddie. I'm not getting into *that*. Now be patient, cherub, and you'll see what I'm getting at. The people in the Valley realized what an Eden they occupied, and successive generations have been content to enjoy their prosperity and maintain the status quo. Unfortunately, population has a way of expanding, and territory does not. And so we have arrived at a crucial point in our history—"

"Eldred, I absolutely forbid you to go on." Edward thumped the table with his fist. "Using this child as a sounding board for your fuzzy dialectics is not only pompous but pointless."

"Oh, control yourself, Eddie. I've warned you about your blood pressure."

Edward turned to Peter with a chilly half-smile. "No offense, young man, but these intramural squabbles which so delight my brother can only bore and confuse you. If you've finished your *mousse au nougatin* we shall excuse you—"

"We shall *not* excuse him," said Dr. El, "until he's heard the case and rendered his verdict."

"Your choise of after-dinner games is deplorable!"

Dr. El's voice became soft and insinuating. "We all have our favorite little games, don't we? If you want me to play yours, you must be patient with mine. Do you understand, Eddie?"

Unexpectedly, this seemed to placate Edward. Dr. El favored Peter with one of his most seductive smiles. "The truth now, cherub. Are we boring you?"

Peter was delighted to cross Edward Breed. "Not at all."

"Then perhaps I may make my point without further interruption?"

"Oh, go to hell!" Edward reached for the decanter and refilled his glass.

"In due time, brother dear, in due time. Now, cherub. The problem is this, and I beg you to keep a perfectly open mind. It's axiomatic that whenever any system of thought is translated into political or social action, its harmless theorists spawn colonies of madly aggressive apostles, bequeathing to them sermons that are promptly turned into ammunition. Are you with me? Farewell speeches and Dead Sea scrolls, diaries and journals, that sort of thing, you know. If you can't have Delphic oracles and burning bushes, you must at least have sacred writings. In this case, Azariah Breed's journals.

"Now, there's nothing that feeds self-righteousness so well as prosperity, and old Azariah, beholding his handiwork, waxed prophetic in his dotage and dreamed in his journals of an Eden stretching far beyond the Brokenstraw Ridge. In the past few years, some of those who have inherited the mantle of authority in this valley have chosen to interpret those senile maunderings as a mandate for action, and with the usual bigoted zeal of apostles are insisting that the present crisis can be resolved by acting upon this imaginary mandate."

He paused, took a lingering sip of water, scowled goodnaturedly at his brother's angry countenance, and continued.

"Of course, the idea is madness. Science has a much simpler answer. Retrenchment, not expansion. Don't you agree it would be more sensible and far safer, cherub?"

Without the essential data which would have made all this comprehensible, Peter was at a complete loss, having learned nothing but that an antagonism divided the brothers, growing apparently out of some obscure conflict over the writings of that nasty old coot badgering them from above the sideboard.

And then he caught a look, rather smug and playful, that passed between the brothers.

They were making fun of him!

He was the butt of a private joke, the pawn in an exchange of wits that was a dialogue, not a duel. Ignoring Dr. El's question, he looked coldly at Edward and asked to be excused from the table.

"You must forgive my brother, young man." A gleam of something like sympathy crept into Edward's wine-fogged eyes. "And don't let him frighten you. He's one of those curious anomalies—a sadist who hates the sight of blood."

Not till the end of the first week of his visit—and how long it was to last he neither inquired nor was told—did he catch a glimpse of Miss Celestia, and then one day she was at the table when he went in to lunch.

She looked neither better nor worse than the last time he'd seen her, but gave the impression of having reached a stage of decrepitude that would progress no further until death itself completed the final stages of decay. Yet she was considerably more listless and withdrawn, and only with a visible effort could she utter a coherent sentence.

In spite of this, Peter still fancied he saw a spark of cunning in her eyes when she saw him enter the room.

Each dish offered to her was shoved aside with a crabby protest: "Swill, swill, swill!"

"Perhaps we're not hungry," purred Edward. "Perhaps we've been nibbling on angel food cake."

This was directed *sotto voce* at Dr. El, but she heard and her voice gathered strength: "My *soul* is nourished by angel food."

Dr. El leaned toward Peter and whispered something about "a touch of arteriosclerotic confusion. Sometimes she even sees Jesus Christ."

While she nodded over the second course, Dr. El teased Peter into telling her what he'd been doing during his visit. She paid no attention until he spoke of the library, and then she said with wheezy urgency, "What books? What books?"

At Dr. El's nudging he mentioned some of his favorite authors, confessing that he was partial to books of memoirs by people who had enjoyed fame and wealth and then suffered catastrophic reverses that left them in poverty, his favorites being actresses and royal mistresses, or in a pinch, composers. He mentioned a book about Chopin he'd found in the library and one he was reading now about the Italian Renaissance, all about the Borgias and Sforzas and Malatestas.

"They were always poisoning each other," he said.

No response. She merely shook her head and said, "Slop, slop, slop."

Peter blushed and looked down at his plate. She must be mad. The rest was his imagination.

"Trollope!" she cried, startling him. *"The Eustace Diamonds!"*

"To each his own, Auntie C.," murmured Dr. El. "I myself must confess to a penchant for mysteries. I've always maintained that Dickens's *Mystery of Edwin Drood*—"

"Garbage, garbage, garbage!"

This time she rapped her knuckles on the table until Peter looked up. *"The Eustace Diamonds.* Remember!" And then, still holding his gaze: "Poetry!"

Peter was at a loss to decipher the message, if indeed

she was trying to convey one. In despair, he mentioned an inscribed copy of *Fleet Street Eclogues* he'd found in the library and which had attracted him by the freshness of its verses and by the knowledge that its author had killed himself.

Again the old lady shook her head, as if vexed and displeased by all these wrong guesses. "Keats? Keats?"

He tried to explain his indifference to Keats. Dr. El sided with him. "I quite agree, cherub. Keats is for moonstruck maidens. Give me someone more—robust. Like Swinburne."

Miss Celestia laughed, as mirthless a sound as old bones rattling in the dark.

"Swinburne. Bah!" Her tone disposed of him more eloquently than decades of critical abuse. Her eyes dredged Peter's face. " 'Hyperion to a satyr!' "

Dr. El started to say something, but she silenced him with a rapid nervous fluttering of her hands, calling suddenly: "Weems!"

In a flash that amazon was through the door and at her side.

"Library! *Complete Poems, Keats and Shelley*. Red binding. Fetch!"

Weems glanced at Edward, who slyly nodded approval. When she came back with the book and was going to hand it to Miss Celestia, the old lady jabbed a finger toward Peter. "Her! Her!"

That took care of lunch, but as she was wheeled past him on her way out Miss Celestia grabbed Peter's arm. Her voice trembled; it might have been weak with fatigue—or taxed with panic: "Swinburne. Keats. 'Hyperion to a satyr!' "

Leafing through the volume later in his room, he attached no significance to Miss Celestia's behavior until his eye chanced upon the title page of one of the longer poems: *Hyperion. A Fragment*.

He was certain she had given him a clue—until he had read through the lines twice without discovering any reason she should have drawn his attention to this particular poem. A coincidence, that's all. A chance connection, logical to a literary mind: Keats and the phrase from *Hamlet*. He threw the book aside. He had to stop imagining things. Face it—she was crazy.

But then he got to thinking about her eyes and the tone of her voice; they haunted him, made him restless and unsatisfied. He went back to the book, reread the poem, scanned the index of first lines, explored the table of contents—

The Fall of Hyperion!

He turned to it quickly and feasted on its metaphors until he felt as if he'd gorged on too many strawberry sundaes. He'd read almost to the end of the first canto, again without finding any hidden meanings, when he turned a page and felt his heart give a skip.

> . . . *and let there be*
> *Beautiful things made new for the surprise*
> *Of the sky children.*

The last three words were firmly underlined in red ink.

They had been at his diary again.

It was shoved too far back among the handkerchiefs, and though it was possible he might have shut the drawer hard enough to have jarred the book into this position, it was more likely that someone had disturbed it.

Now he could understand why it had been returned to him: whoever had stolen it or caused it to be stolen in the first place was hopeful of keeping tabs on his discoveries, should he make any more, by sneaking looks at the diary.

But why alert him by stealing it at all? Why hadn't the thief simply read it and left it where it was?

Maybe it had had to be delivered to someone at the Abbey for examination, which would mean there must be at least two people involved; the thief at the farm and the instigator at the Abbey.

He was frightened, but also angry enough to think of setting a trap for them with a false entry:

Have found out about the sky children.

It had to mean something. Miss Celestia had purposely drawn his attention to the phrase.

A single hair strategically placed against the cover would tell him if anyone moved the diary again.

The following day, he stayed clear of his room for hours at a time and didn't go upstairs till late in the evening.

He carefully opened the drawer and saw at once that

the diary had been moved. He looked around the room, tense and shivery, as if the intruder were still there.

He wrote to his mother telling her he wanted to come home right away, but since Hadleigh took the mail to be posted, he had no way of being sure she would get it.

In a pink-flowered maternity dress, Welcome looked more than ever like a valentine; he was so glad to see her he scarcely noticed the massive bulge of her belly.

"I thought they were lying. I thought I'd never see you again."

"You look bigger," she said.

"So do you." He didn't even blush.

She looked down at herself. "Awful, isn't it, lovey? Oh, well, not much longer. Any hour."

Peter decided he'd better talk fast. Besides, Dr. El had warned him when he took him to this remote room in the east wing that he mustn't stay more than a few minutes.

"Welcome, listen to me. I've only got—"

"And what a gorgeous tan you've got."

"Not like Krieg's. Welcome—"

"How is Krieg—and everyone?"

He wasn't sure the pause marked any distinction of affection. "They're fine. But what about you? I've been so worried about you."

"What for? I'm strong as an ox."

"I mean—" He didn't want to alarm her. "I was afraid something might have happened to you."

"Like what?"

This was no good. There wasn't time to hedge. "I thought they might have done something to you."

"*Done* something?"

"Punished you."

"Whatever for, lovey?"

Her complete innocence made his concern seem childish; there was no way he could communicate that shadowy feeling of *wrongness*.

"Welcome, tell me the truth. Is he your father?"

"Who?"

"Edward Breed."

The answer flashed across her face in a glow of merriment, and he said quickly, "Or your guardian?"

"No, of course not!"

He told her what he'd overheard the day Edward Breed had come to tea at Aunt Affie's.

She could not have been more amused if he had told her a very funny joke. "The only reason I'm here, lovey, is that Dr. El wanted me to have special care before the baby was born. So here I am." She swept her arm around the comfortable room. "And I *love* it!"

The theft of his diary couldn't be laughed away; he told her about that.

Though she didn't laugh, she was plainly skeptical. "Now, who would want to read your diary?" And then, as if sensing she'd given offense, "Not that it wouldn't be very interesting. The secret life of Peter Patrick!"

Her refusal to share his concern began to annoy him. "I'm sure it's got something to do with the sky children."

A bee drifted through the open window; she seemed more intent on watching its lazy buzzing circle of the room than in listening to him. "The *what*, lovey?"

"Sky children. It must mean something." He told her about Miss Celestia and *The Fall of Hyperion.*

She touched his arm. "She's gone loony. You must have noticed that. Everyone knows it."

When he persisted, she began to pout. "Dr. El brought you up here to cheer me *up*, lovey."

His stubborn, wounded silence moved her to give him a hug.

"You've imagined all this, lovey. I suppose I'd get the same ideas if I was to be plunked down in some city with a whole lot of strange people."

He couldn't deny he'd imagined the dreadful things they had done to her; here she was, bright as a new star and carefree as a child.

There had been no sound in the passage, but suddenly Dr. El was at the door.

"Sorry, pets. Visiting hours are over. Don't frown, cherub. Perhaps tomorrow you may stay longer."

Welcome followed them to the door. "I'm being spoiled, Dr. El."

"Beauty's privilege," he murmured. "Enjoy it, my dear."

Shortly after midnight, a scream woke him up.

It was followed by a low, gurgling murmur which at first he thought must have come from outside the house. It came again as he looked out the window. Then he knew it must have come from the floor above, from a room whose window must be directly above his.

As he waited, listening, a baby squalled its first greeting to the world.

Welcome's baby!

He waited impatiently for Edward and Dr. El at the breakfast table next morning, anxious to find out if Welcome was all right; surely all that prenatal coddling must have foreshadowed some grave concern.

Dr. El came in looking unusually sleek, palm-brushing his hair with sweepingly vigorous strokes and dismissing Peter's anxiety with a smile. "My dear cherub, she couldn't be better."

Edward, trailing after him, looked at Peter coolly. "Why do you ask?"

Peter stared at him. "I heard the baby—last night when it was born! Was it a boy?"

Some of the brightness went out of Dr. El's face. Edward worked his jaws and looked gloomy. "Alas," said Dr. El, spreading his napkin, "it was."

Peter swallowed. "Was?"

Dr. El gravely stirred his coffee. "Died at birth."

"But I heard it this morning, too." What were they up to now?

The brothers looked at him in unison, then at each other. Then they both ventured careful smiles devoid of any unseemly glitter of teeth.

"That was another baby, cherub. You'll be pleased to learn that my brother became the father of a healthy baby boy last night. Isn't that wonderful?"

Peter thought it was an odd time for them to be making fun of him.

"The girl Welcome remains in blooming health," said Edward morosely, "while her poor baby dies. My Marguerite bears a healthy child and then slips herself into the Dark Embrace."

To add to the outrageousness of this nonsense, the two monstrous liars sat there placidly stuffing their mouths with huge, syrupy omelettes.

"Who's Marguerite?"

Their eyes remained meekly downcast. Edward prodded his flabby mouth with a napkin. "My wife. Yes. I'm sorry you weren't favored with her acquaintance—"

"She was ill," put in Dr. El.

58

"A nervous debility. She was afflicted with a profound—horror—of society."

"She would see no one," added Dr. El. "Only Eddie."

"For years." Edward's tone was morbid.

Dr. El looked up, as if from prayer. "In the garden, cherub, did you perchance ever look up and see a face like a lily at the farthest window in the west wing?"

"With golden hair," said Edward helpfully. "Like an angel's halo."

"You didn't? Ah . . ."

An angel-haired lily languishing in the west wing? Even Peter's overly romantic imagination boggled at this.

"She was indeed an angel," lamented Dr. El, "by which I mean a very superior being."

"The world was too rude for her."

"Its touch, its glance, sickened her."

"Eddie, remember the time we were marooned in a snowstorm on our way back to Brokenstraw and had to take refreshment at a roadside restaurant?"

"A vulgar establishment, as I recall."

"Vulgar but respectable. It was all we could do to get poor Marguerite through the door. She cowered between us at a corner table."

"There was one of those vile jukeboxes."

"The waitress was a gross creature, the cuisine even less inspiring. In an itsy-bitsy voice, you could hardly hear her, Marguerite said, 'I'd like a wiener sandwich, please.' "

Edward sighed. "She was so refined."

"The waitress smirked; and when she was in the middle of that crowded room—full of truck drivers and that sort—she turned and yelled back at Marguerite: 'Hey, lady! Watcha want on that dog?' Poor Marguerite. She fainted dead away."

"It was the last time she ever left her rooms."

Peter could think of only one suitable response to this: in absolute silence, he picked up his fork and began to eat.

Welcome looked only mildly startled when Peter slipped into her room like a fugitive, pressing a finger to his lips.

Three days had gone by before Edward's and Dr. El's absence from the house had given him a chance to sneak up to Welcome's room, where he found her sitting on a stool by the window embroidering a pillowcase. Although paler than when he'd seen her last, and with bluish smudges under her eyes, her valentine smile was as cheery as ever.

She started chattering at once, waving the pillowcase before his eyes with childish pride. Taken aback, he let her go on till she stopped. Then he said, "But, Welcome, what about the baby?"

She jumped up and did a little pirouette to show off her slim figure. "See for yourself! It's gone!"

"I know."

"*You* don't sound very pleased, lovey."

Her carefree manner dumbfounded him. "That night—I heard you scream—"

"Did I? I guess so. Then dear Dr. El gave me a shot and everything went blank."

Was it possible she hadn't been told? But no, she saw the look on his face and hastened to say, "I suppose you heard, didn't you? The poor little doll-baby died."

He held back an angry protest, shocked that even if she believed it to be true, she could take it so calmly.

"I must say, Welcome, you don't seem too terribly upset."

She looked vaguely puzzled. "Should I be?"

"Don't you *know*?"

"Lovey, why are you staring at me like that?"

She looked genuinely perplexed, as if it really were a doll they were talking about and his concern about it ridiculous.

"Well, *say* something," she pleaded. "You mad at me?"

The awful part of it was that he couldn't detect the faintest gleam of duplicity in her lively eyes—only an innocent, wounded bewilderment.

"I don't understand you," he said.

"What's so hard to understand about me?"

"Listen, Welcome. Your baby's not dead. It's downstairs at the other end of the house, in the nursery."

She couldn't have been less surprised. "Not *my* baby, lovey. My baby died."

"It did not! You wouldn't be sitting there grinning like a monkey if it had."

She gave him a long, worried look full of affection. "You shouldn't take things so hard, lovey."

"Welcome!"

"But, lovey, it's only a baby. A dead baby."

An emotional side effect of the shock of losing the baby. Or else—

"Are you glad? Is that it?"

"That the baby died? Oh, no!"

"I guess it does solve your problem."

"What problem, lovey?"

His patience snapped. "As if you don't know! You had a baby. He didn't have a father. One you were married to, I mean. I may be young, but I'm not an idiot. If the baby died, it would remove that particular problem. Right? But it's not very nice to—*rejoice* about it. Besides, the baby's alive. I know right where it is down there in—"

"So do I, smarty."

"Oh?"

"In the garbage can."

His lips felt the shock.

She giggled. "Well, it is. Or else it's down there in the garden under one of them rosebushes. Who cares? It's over and done with, and I'm glad!"

Very distinctly, he said, "Your baby is *alive*."

"Dead."

"Alive."

"Dead."

"Alive!"

"Dead!"

"Welcome, stop that!"

"It's dead." The amused, pouting defiance of a child intent upon having the last word.

"Listen. Edward told me he had a wife named Marguerite. Nobody's laid eyes on her for ages, according to him and Dr. El. They told me all this the next morning. They said she had a baby the same night you did. What do you think of that?"

"Boy or girl?"

"A boy! And then his wife's supposed to have died!"

"That's too bad."

"Welcome!"

"Well, it is. Maybe you better go, lovey. Everything I say makes you mad."

"What do I have to do to get through to you? It's all too fantastic—can't you see that? Now tell me the truth." He fixed her with one of Daddy's most severe let's-cut-out-the-nonsense looks. "Was Edward Breed your baby's father?"

"A while ago you thought he was *my* father."

"Answer my question."

"I'm not sure, lovey. I was drugged."

"Not when he was born. I mean—"

"I know what you mean. It's true. I went to sleep one night and had the most wonderful deep sleep. Oh, for hours longer than usual. And I had all sorts of *dreams*. And that's the night it happened."

She might have been describing how to make rosettes, and it was this total lack of shame, stemming not from callousness—that was clear to him now—but from an innocence incalculably more profound than his own, that made his heart melt toward her. He must be kind to her. She must be humored and guarded.

"And this happened at Aunt Affie's?"

She shrugged. "I guess so."

"Don't you know?"

She looked exactly like a child guilty of some trivial misdemeanor. "I guess so. Yes."

He felt a burning hatred for *them*—whoever it was who had done this vile thing to poor Welcome, turned her into a creature whose normal maternal instinct had been paralyzed. How had they done it? By what trick, drug, or evil influence? He longed to press her valentine face against his cheek and soothe away—what? She was devoid of fear and shame and grief, her emotions curiously deadened. Again he thought of Krieg, how much alike they were.

"Would you like to see it, Welcome?"

"See what?"

"Your baby!"

"Who'd want to see a dead baby?"

"You come with me. I'll show you how dead he is."

She didn't move. "Lovey, you're going to get us both in a heap of trouble."

Was she afraid? So afraid she didn't dare show it, not even to him?

"Your baby's in a nursery downstairs. I saw it. Now come on."

"Not me. Dr. El gave me orders to stay in my room. When you've had a baby, lovey, you don't just get up and fly around."

"You're scared, aren't you?"

"Don't be silly."

"Then come on."

"But it's so stupid, lovey. Everyone's quite happy with things like they are. What do you have to be such a nuisance for?"

He told himself to be gentle, not to lose patience. "You're working for Aunt Affie and one day somebody comes along and drugs you and does nasty, dirty things to you and you end up having a baby that's stolen from you—and you're *happy?*"

"Don't be such a prude, lovey."

"You're sick, that's what you are."

"I told you. I can't leave the room."

"Dr. El won't see you. He and Edward both went out. But we've got to hurry."

With a look of bored resignation, she gave in. "It's all your fault if we get caught."

They were not caught. They were not even seen, thanks to Peter's skill at reconnoitering the area before they ventured into it. In five minutes, they were standing beside the elaborate crib in a nursery that was both a masterpiece and a nightmare of cloudy blue opulence.

Alone in the room, the bonneted baby slumbered peacefully.

Peter reached for Welcome's hand. "Be quiet, now, and look at him. He's *your* baby."

Welcome beamed down at the wizened pink face. "Sweet little doll-baby," she cooed.

Like the character in Trollope, Peter loathed baby worship, but he rejoiced at this. "You mustn't pick him up."

Now she'd seen the baby, he was afraid she might insist on whisking him away with her, which would create quite another problem; he had visions of the two of them spiriting the baby away through the woods, pursued by the man with the German shepherd.

Supposing they did get away, would Krieg help them?

"Don't worry, I won't," said Welcome in a pawky tone certainly not that of a mother about to snatch her baby out of the grasp of fiends.

He gave her hand a hard squeeze. "Welcome, it's *your* baby."

"Oh, do quit saying that, lovey. My baby died."

"*This* is your baby."

She had already lost interest in it. "Come on, let's get out of here. Somebody'll catch us and tell Dr. El."

He looked despairingly from her to the baby, wishing

there were some marked resemblance he might call to her attention, but the baby looked discouragingly nondescript. Finally, there was nothing to do but follow her back to her room.

On the threshold, she paused and put her hand on his arm.

"You'd better not come in, lovey. I'm supposed to be resting."

"Welcome, *believe* me. The baby—"

"Is sweet as pie and just adorable. But he's not mine."

"He *is!*"

She touched his cheek. "You're sweet and adorable, too, to want to cheer me up. But really—I'm fine. These things happen." Her tone was the ghastliest travesty of grief. He was confused and angry and helpless.

"They happen here. No place else. Edward Breed wanted an heir. You've been *used*—that's all. It's heartless and vicious. Now I suppose he'll just send you away—or do something even worse."

"Back to the farm, I hope," she said complacently. "Keep your fingers crossed, lovey."

Suddenly the radiance went out of her smile; she looked as if she might cry. Finally, it might be reaching her.

"Do I really?" she said, genuinely woeful.

"What?"

"Look like a monkey?"

He gave up. "I didn't say that."

"Maybe you don't want to see me again."

"Don't be silly."

Affectionately, but not quite as a sister would have done it, she slid a hand around his neck and teased the short hairs above his collar. "Know something, lovey? You seem lots older to me now than you did at Mrs. Juul's. I thought you were such a baby then."

He consciously deepened his voice. "Now look, Welcome. I want to help you. But I can't if you won't help me."

"How can I?"

"Is there any way you could get a message to Miss Celestia?"

"Without Weems knowing it? What do you think?"

"I've got to let her know that I know she's trying to tell me something."

"Oh, lovey, not that again."

"I've got to find out about the sky children."

"It's all a game—a joke—"

"I don't believe that."

She leaned away from him. "Maybe you're just trying to get me into trouble. Maybe they've put you up to all this."

"That's crazy!"

"Word of honor?"

"Word of honor."

"Seal it with a kiss?"

The light in her eyes when she said this made him feel shaky and excited. Her face with its cinnamon-candy lips was almost touching his; the closer it came the more severe became his expression; when she actually kissed him, his face was puckered into a tight frown; while *inside*...

"Nice," she whispered. "Nicer if you kissed me back."

She shut her eyes, and tilted her head. Peter took her awkwardly by the shoulders and kissed her on the lips. Before he could draw back, her hand was behind his head, pushing him closer.

The feel of her tongue in his mouth was as shocking, in its way, as a bee sting, and when it delved deeper, moist and caressive, he began to reel.

"Mmmm ... much nicer, lovey."

Brick-red, he stammered something about not having known many girls.

"I'm glad," she murmured.

"Are you?"

"You're a very good-looking boy."

"Not like Krieg," he mumbled stupidly.

"Better."

"He's—"

"An ox. I like sweet lambs, like you." She opened the door. "Better go now, lovey."

He felt he'd both gained and lost ground. "Please, Welcome. Think about what I said. About the baby."

She reached out and pinched his cheek the way Aunt Affie might have done.

"Oh, you and your old baby!"

He went back to this room sadly confused.

Lying on the bed he became once more absorbed in the study of his own face in the hand mirror, certain, like Dorian Gray, that this momentous experience must have left its mark, and wondering if it was actually possible Welcome could prefer him to Krieg. He had to admit it was a rather nice face, if it happened to be the sort that appealed to you. It wasn't streaky or blemished, and had good lines and fair, fresh coloring.

He slid the tip of his tongue forward till it was just visible, moist and pink, and he thought with a sexual thrill of the exciting uses to which this hitherto private part of his body could be put—this and other private parts. For once he thought of his body not as an object of contempt, but as a source of pleasures yet to be explored. He wondered what Welcome would look like undressed.

His tongue touched its image in the glass, and for the next half hour he devoted himself earnestly to the practice of kissing.

The sun, hardly warmer than the moon, crept up the back of the sky with promises of another glorious morning in the Valley. This, or something else, had put Dr. El in a gleeful mood, and he drove the big Packard along the country lanes with such abandon Peter was sorry he'd come along; nor would he have if he hadn't been taken so completely by surprise. It was the first time Dr. El had ever asked him to go with him on his rounds.

Between stops, Dr. El would chatter about inconsequential things, and when he did call at two or three farms he always told Peter to stay in the car, almost as if an epidemic were raging among the hills and the houses were full of pestilence. By midmorning he was therefore bored and angry, and also hungry as noon drew near, but then, instead of heading straight back to the Abbey for lunch, Dr. El took what he called "a little detour on the way back," which turned out to be an hour-long ride deep into the hills.

The wildness of the countryside and Dr. El's silence began to make Peter uneasy. They finally stopped at the foot of a sloping stretch of meadow, yellow with mustard and fringed with poison sumac. Here Dr. El urged him out of the car—"to stretch our legs"—and up the slope till they came to where a chorus of blackbirds sang in a grove of poplars. They paused to listen and then continued uphill to a sort of dell below the ridge where the ground was unexpectedly littered with tombstones, some of them so old as to be unreadable.

A long way to bring anyone to be buried, Peter thought.

An indefinable but sharper anxiety made him forget that he was hungry.

Dr. El motioned him to sit down on one of the granite slabs. Around them the poplars trembled and whispered under the cloudless blue sky; their leaves, like the silver wafers of the money plant in Aunt Affie's backyard, glinted in the summer breeze. Far below, distance gave an illusion of neatness to the patchwork fields. The nearest farm was too far away to be seen.

Dr. El called his attention to the largest monument, set apart from the others by a rusty iron fence. A wingless angel reclined against a granite column, its features soft as soap in the green shadows of a sycamore tree. The name on the base was Azariah Breed; this was the resting place of that mettlesome patriarch.

As Dr. El talked, Peter noticed a suppressed nervous excitement about him as he rummaged about and lit a cigarette. Peter had never seen him smoke before, and he did it so oddly it might have been the first time he had, pinching and puffing and uttering decorous graveyard coughs as if a funeral were in progress a few feet away.

"Would you believe, my dear cherub, that I know every stone and tree and brook down there. Ah, yes, I know it all—

'Where once my careless childhood strayed,
A stranger yet to pain!'

"You haven't forgotten your Thomas Gray, I trust. Oh, cherub, cherub, how I envy you! Only as children are we ever truly, *truly* free. Did you ever think of that? You will, someday, much sooner than you think. Do you know *why* children are free? I shall tell you."

With the air of imparting a confidence, he brought his lips close to Peter's ear. "It's obedience that makes one free, cherub. That's one of life's great secrets. And one of its ironies. You have a father who is the god omnipotent of your little world; as long as you remain obedient to him, you'll be spared the 'heavy and the weary weight of all this unintelligible world.'"

He paused and gravely squashed out his cigarette. "Why this perpetual bleating clamor for *freedom* and *escape*? Could it be, cherub, that we all know there's neither escape nor freedom and so we treasure these two delusions above all others, even above God and Love? Listen to Nietzsche—'Art thou one *entitled* to escape from a yoke? Many a one hath cast away his final worth when he hath cast away his servitude.' Think about *that*."

A cloud of foreboding settled upon Peter. He was sure this was why Dr. El had brought him up here ... But why? What was the deeper purpose?

"The most lasting works of art in the Western world were acts of pure obedience. Obedience, which is not the expression of faith but its very keystone. We don't obey that which we believe so much as we believe that which we obey. When man ceased to obey God, art declined into decoration. When you cease to obey your father, cherub, he'll no longer be a god, but only your 'old man.'

"Freedom can be the most destructive condition in the human experience. It can render one's life aimless and wasteful. For your own amusement, cherub, postulate a condition of society where there are those who command and those who obey, without repression to the body nor discomfort to the soul. Which do you think would be more truly free? Those who command? Not at all. Obedience is the key to freedom.

"Who, you may well ask, is to decide who shall command and who shall obey? The only possible answer is that it must be an arbitrary decision. Nor is this as immoral as it may sound, for in determining who is to live and who is to die, is not nature wholly arbitrary? Are the good spared and the evil laid low? Are the brave given long lives and the corrupt cut down?

"No, indeed. Nature, in her infinite wisdom, which is to know there can be no wisdom, is supremely, blindly, mercifully arbitrary, and there is no appealing her arbitrariness. So must it be with freedom, that most relative of all human values.

"There's really nothing new in all this. Carlyle sums it up very neatly somewhere. Ah, cherub, how my soul yearns for the end of all this, which will be a new and vital faith. Oh, not the old, holy hocus-pocus, but faith in a doctrine of dynamic animism, which is to know that the essence of life is immaterial spirit, that the body is a mere husk, a functionary, a tool."

His voice lingered over the last word, caressed it as his long white fingers sketched the air, and then, as if pursuing a quite different thread of thought, he smiled at Peter with maidenly coyness. "Forgive me for boring you, cherub. It's just that I come here quite often to meditate—usually upon my sins. At the moment, however, there's a less sublime function I really must attend to. I shan't be long."

He got up and then paused, looking down at Peter with a naughtily expectant air. "Care to watch, cherub?"

Peter was too horrified to do more than rudely shake his head and look quickly in the other direction, looking around again only when Dr. El disappeared among the fir trees near the top of the ridge.

Alone and glad of it, Peter couldn't resist the not unpleasant wave of sadness that rolled over him and seemed, more than the wind, to be what sighed among the poplars and set last year's leaves to rustling among the tombstones. He didn't like the place and wanted to get away from it.

Dr. El, perhaps out of spite, was certainly taking his time about it.

At length his absence began to seriously alarm Peter. He was struck by an awesomely terrifying thought:

What if Dr. El had done a disappearing act?

The morning's routine became suddenly sinister. Why, on this particular morning and never before, had Dr. El urged him to come along on his rounds?

Nerves tingling, he jumped up and looked all around him, knowing what it would mean to be stranded so far from any house, encircled by rugged woods and perilous terrain through which he'd never in a million years find his way back to the Abbey. He wouldn't even know which way to go.

A simple way to find out if his predicament was real would be to retrace his steps down the slope till he could see if the car was still parked beside the road. But if he were to do that and the car *wasn't* there... It was a moment of truth he preferred to postpone, and so he waited, his mind full of night thoughts, bears, wolves, snakes, and swamps, quicksand and pitfalls.

If they wanted to get rid of him, he was sure this was the way they'd go about it.

At last he got up and started slowly up the ridge toward the firs near the top, and as he neared the crest he became aware of a sound so faint as to be hardly audible at first: a muffled, plangent hammering that grew louder and was mingled with the sound of shouting and laughter.

There was no sign of Dr. El at the top of the ridge, but

he could look down into a broad ravine upon a sight so fantastic and unexpected he couldn't at first believe it was real:

Below him through the valley railroad tracks severed the countryside, and the sounds he'd heard came from a gang of section hands at work repairing the tracks.

At first glance, the workmen were only a welter of blue-clad legs and brown torsos, but as he watched he could pick out an arm, a back, a pair of shoulders, the dazzling brutish arrogance of a face uplifted to the scorching sun.

Intense relief made it the most beautiful sight Peter had ever seen.

Their voices rose, a burst of some coarse song yodeled upward, and presently he saw one of them drop his pickax and stride across the tracks as if intent on scaling the embankment, but instead stopping beside the ditch running between the bank and tracks and roughly, boyishly, with a clowning, virile swagger, spread his legs and pissed into the weeds.

At that moment, Peter heard a muffled cry from close at hand. Startled, he looked along the edge of the ridge and caught the sudden jerky movement of an arm among the mustard plants. He hurried toward it.

There, stretched out among the burdocks and milkweed and mustard, his white suit wrinkled and twisted and soiled with grass stains, lay Dr. El on his stomach.

Peter had never felt so ashamed. While he had dawdled down below, imagining himself abandoned, poor Dr. El must have been lying here stricken—maybe even dying—and wondering why *he* had been abandoned. Peter rushed to his side.

Dr. El spotted him and gave an oddly savage snarl of surprise, his body flopping and twisting like a wounded snake's. Peter froze, astonished by the look of rage on the man's normally placid features and dumbfounded at the sight of his immaculate trousers wrenched down around his knees. Turning aside in shame, he stared down at the workmen Dr. El must have been watching as he'd made cheerless love to the ground.

"Nosy little bastard! Sticking your goddamn snotty nose into everything! Go on—get out of here! Sneaky little son of a bitch! Snoop! Pest!"

Aghast, Peter turned and fled down through the

graveyard and the whispering poplars, out of which at his headlong flight a cloud of blackbirds swept skyward in a long, trailing arc. He reached the car and leaned panting against it.

"Oh, brother!" he said aloud, gasping. "Oh, *brother!*"

Getting his breath back, he walked aimlessly back and forth along the road, darting anxious glances up the slope, and finally, sweaty and exhausted, crawled into the car itself and waited in the bakery-oven heat for the unexpected.

At length the skinny, soiled figure of Dr. El came strolling calmly down the slope. As he came closer, Peter could see how neatly he had knotted his tie and how tidily his trousers and jacket had been brushed free of sticks and grass. Even the wrinkles had almost vanished, leaving only faint lines on the linen, just as all signs of emotion had been smoothed out his face.

"Sorry to be so long, cherub."

Getting in, he ducked his head to squint at himself in the mirror, patting a few stray hairs into place and spit-washing his eyebrows.

"Shall we call it a day?" he said breezily. "This heat's too tiresome for anything but breathing."

Astonished beyond words at the man's composure, Peter felt oddly distrustful of his own impressions of what he'd seen and heard. It seemed necessary to concentrate on remembering the road back to the Abbey, keeping in mind how far they strayed from the railroad tracks. He had to be able to find them again.

Only in dreams had he ever felt so helplessly frightened.

Fear made him hold his tongue, nor could he have talked anyway to a man who had become so complex a character, a dual personality—dual or triple or even more, for all he knew.

For that matter, how many Welcomes were there? How many Kriegs? How many Aunt Affies?

How many Peter Patricks?

Peter Patricks, one after another, stretched ahead of him in his mind like hitchhikers along the road, variously dressed—some smiling, some frowning, some wrinkled and weary and cynical. There they all stood, waiting for him to take possession, buried somewhere within him really, hidden mercifully beneath layers of skin and experience, and deepest of all—at this point nearly unimaginable—an old, tired, wizened, possibly crippled, hopeless and helpless dodderer, and when all the other layers had been peeled off by time, there he would stand at last, the end of the line of Peter Patricks. And between the Peter Patrick he was now and this crochety, cranky stranger, what would his eyes see? Where would his feet travel? What inconceivable sights and distances lay ahead?

The immediate prospect was blurred by a fog of deepening terror.

There was a letter from Mother waiting for him at the Abbey:

Dear Peter,

Daddy and I have been feeling so much better after getting your jolly letter. Naturally, you would be a little homesick at first, but we're glad that's over and you're having such a good time. Aunt Affie's letter cheered us, too. What a grand old lady she must be!

We shall have to inquire around for the nearest riding stables so you can keep up this healthful sport when you get home. You've no idea how pleased Daddy was to hear about *that*. He's proud as a peacock—and so am I, darling.

Well, I haven't got much news. The Fourth Street Bridge is reopened to traffic, thank goodness. It's a pleasure to go downtown again without going halfway around the moon. Daddy and I are going to the Little Theater with Mr. and Mrs. Strong, new members of the Lodge. Speaking of which, I hung the new curtains in the Lodge, but they were so heavy we have to get new rods. Daddy hasn't a free moment now that he's Exalted Ruler (or *Exhausted Rooster* as I like to call him when he gets too high and mighty.)

Must stop now as Mrs. Morrissey is here to take me for groceries. With all our love, angel,

Mother

His *jolly* letter?

Somewhere he must have taken the wrong turn; the passages all looked alike, but he was sure Welcome's room was closer to the stairs. He was about to turn back when he heard voices up ahead around the corner. There were lights up that way, and as he crept forward he could distinguish Edward's sharp, peremptory tones. Afraid to go any nearer, he stood where he was in the dark passageway and listened. It sounded like an argument.

"I want the truth, do you hear? Did you pull something with that kid?"

"*Pull* something?"

Dr. El!

"It won't do. I won't have it. He's not one of them, you know."

"Be a dear, Eddie, and hand me that flask. No, no. The big one."

"This change of heart is awfully sudden. I don't trust it."

"Anyone would think you weren't pleased. Furthermore, my dear Eddie, it is hardly a *change* of anything. I never said I was categorically opposed to your little—project. I merely insisted upon sufficient preliminary research."

"Which you completed this afternoon?"

"I decided it would work, yes."

"Well, something must have decided you."

"Of course. I've satisfied myself there's an area of susceptibility."

"Meaning what?"

"The subject would have to be suggestible, or it wouldn't have a prayer."

"What are you so fidgety about?"

"Because you're *hovering* over me!"

"Goddamn it, El! What happened?"

"I told you."

"I saw the way you looked, sneaking up here without a word!"

"Be careful, Eddie."

"I want to know—"

"All *right!* If you must know, the little beast insulted me."

"How?"

"That's neither here nor there."

"*How,* damn you!"

"Really, Eddie, you ought to have been a Jesuit."

"Exactly how did he insult you?"

"He was rude. Impertinent—"

"What did he do?"

"It's what he said."

"What did he say?"

73

"Eddie, I refuse to be cross-examined like this."

"You bloody fool! If you've done anything to queer this thing, I'll wring your skinny neck!"

"Don't threaten me—I warn you! I've had quite enough of your abuse. If you don't leave me alone, I'll never get this done."

Edward's tone became morbidly curious. "Is that it you've got there?"

"One of them."

"All right. I'll go. But you must promise me there's been no hanky-panky. I won't stand for it."

Dr. El giggled. "I declare, one might almost think you were jealous."

"Christ!"

"Forgive me. How could I forget your devotion to *Marguerite?*"

"Grow up, you fool."

"I have, brother dear. Alas, I have. And of all the elixirs I've managed to extract from these 'baleful weeds and precious juiced flowers,' I've never found one that would reverse or stay that process."

"Stick with what you can do. I'll settle for that."

"Then run along, Eddie, and leave me with my potions."

A shadow fell across the light, and Peter slipped back down the passageway.

Daybreak found him hard at work upon a rude map, wholly conjectural in its plotting of distances. He'd made a mark for Brokenstraw, one for Plato Switch, one for Sugar Hill, one for the Abbey, and one for the graveyard. Then he'd drawn in the railroad tracks, which, if his estimate was right, was closer than he'd thought. A point in his favor. And with all those curves, the mail train would slow down long before it reached Plato Switch.

Actually hopping aboard the train would be another matter—easy enough in his mind, but being there and doing it—that might be something else. He would worry about that when the time came.

There was no other way. He had to get in touch with Mother and Daddy, and to do that he must get to Plato Switch. Such an enterprise could hardly be more risky than staying here and pretending nothing was wrong.

Whatever they were up to, it had to be motivated by more than a fear of scandal, and he was involved, just as deeply as Welcome or Miss Celestia or anyone else. Perhaps more deeply.

He hadn't intended to say anything to Welcome, assuming that even if she did agree to go with him—he did hate the thought of leaving her here alone—she was hardly in condition yet to scramble across miles of rugged countryside. But when he saw her in the garden, looking quite as blooming as any of the flowers, he felt he should at least give her the chance.

"I finally talked Dr. El into letting me out of that beastly room," she said.

He tried as adroitly as possible to steer her away from any of the gardeners.

"I thought you liked it."

"I did, lovey. But after a week of it, I was ready to knock down the walls."

"Welcome, now that you've had time to think about the baby and everything—"

"No! If you're going to start that again I'm not going another step with you."

"Okay, I won't."

"Not a word?"

"Not a word."

He led her into the maze. No one could possibly hear them or see them behind these tall hedges of beech and yew. "There's one thing you've got to know, Welcome."

"If it's about that baby—"

"It's about you."

"Lovey, we'll get lost in here. Take my hand."

"Now listen to me, Welcome. This is serious."

"That's the trouble with you, lovey. You take everything so serious."

"Well, this is, believe me. It's a matter of life and death."

"If you dragged me into this spooky place to scare me—"

"Welcome, you should be scared. I am. I'm scared to death. There's something awfully funny going on around here. I've heard things. Scary things."

"I know, lovey. Somebody stole your diary and—"

"It's more than that. It's something worse. Something evil."

"I know what's the matter with you," she said, giving his hand a reproving squeeze. "It's this house. All those gloomy rooms. And places like this. Ugh. It gives me the creeps, too, lovey. Don't think I won't be glad to get back to the farm where I belong."

"It's more than that. You've got to believe me. They're up to something. All of them. I don't know what it is. But it's got something to do with us. We're in danger! I know we are."

She refused to catch any of his anxiety. She seemed uncannily immune to alarm.

"From what?"

"That's just it, Welcome. I don't know."

"Well, lovey, if it's all that vague, why worry?"

"You honestly don't believe me, do you?"

"I don't think you're lying. I don't mean that. I think you're bored and homesick and like to make believe."

"Thanks a lot."

"Now don't be grumpy. You're always telling me to listen. Now you listen for a change. There's nothing wrong with being homesick. I'm homesick for the farm. But you're so afraid of admitting anything like that. Any weakness. You've got a terrible inferiority complex, lovey. You really have. Look how you're always talking about Krieg. Just because he's bigger and stronger than you, you think he's some kind of god. So instead of just coming out and admitting that you're homesick and want to go home, you make believe you're in some kind of danger and really *should* go home before something terrible happens."

"But that doesn't explain all these funny things that have happened."

"You mean your diary and all that."

"I like the way you just *dismiss* everything. As if it's nothing."

"Lovey, you're making something out of nothing."

They were in the center of the maze. "Well, here's something I haven't told you. I wrote home all about it. I mean, I told them I didn't like it here. It was making me worse instead of better, and I wanted to come home. I got Mother's answer yesterday. She was glad I'd written such a *jolly letter!*"

"Then she must have got it."

He couldn't resist giving her a little shake. "But there was nothing the least bit *jolly* about it!"

"Well, maybe it sounded jolly to her."

"Sure, maybe it did sound jolly when she got it. After someone got hold of it and edited it before it was sent."

"Lovey, I've never heard of anything so silly. Let's go back. This place gives me the collywobbles."

"It isn't silly, and I'm going to prove it."

"How?"

"By getting another letter out to Mother. Or maybe a telegram. Or maybe I can phone her. From Plato Switch."

She pulled at his arm to make him stop. "What are you talking about, lovey?"

He lowered his voice. "The railroad isn't too far from here. I'm going to sneak over there and hitch a ride on one of the trains into Plato Switch. It's the only way I can get there."

"Are you *crazy?* You can't do that!"

"If you're smart, you'll come with me."

"Never. Why, I've never heard of anything so crazy."

"Come with me, Welcome. I'll prove to you I'm not just imagining all this."

"The only thing you'll prove to me, lovey, is that you're stark staring mad. Now get that idea right out of your mind."

"I've got to do it, Welcome. You mustn't tell them. Swear to me you won't tell them."

"It would serve you right if I did."

"Promise me you won't."

"Don't worry, I won't. If you want to go to all that trouble and risk to find out you've imagined the whole thing, you go right ahead."

She wouldn't talk to him after that, and when he tried to hold her hand, she pulled it away.

The next morning he was in the garden again, alone, trying to convey as best he could an impression of being unutterably bored and not knowing what to do with himself. From there he went into the library and idled away another half hour and then, carrying his paint set and sketchbook, he wandered into the park with an air of looking for something to paint.

He sat down under an oak tree whose gnarled branches screened from view all but one corner of the Abbey's east wing, which he began to sketch until he felt confident that he had deceived any hidden watchful eye as to his true purpose in being there. He heard nothing and saw no one.

It was a hot day with only the faintest breeze; the gathering opacity of the sky presaged possible afternoon showers. By then, if all went well, he would be in Plato Switch.

Presently he got up, stretched, left his equipment on the ground—a necessary sacrifice—and ambled deeper into the park, hearing nothing but the twittering of birds. He came to the fence marking the eastern boundary of the park, climbed over it, and plunged into the woods.

After walking a few yards, he paused and looked back, feeling for only an instant the barest pressure of indecision before glancing at his rough map and running on again, hopefully straight toward the railroad tracks.

He had gone far enough to exhaust his first wind when, stopping for a breather, he heard the dog.

Or dogs. From the noise of their barking, it might have been a pack. They weren't close enough to cause him any real alarm, only a heart-tripping uneasiness that brought the sweat gushing from his already overheated body. He stopped long enough to rip off his wet shirt and tie it around his waist. Even in this dense shade, the clotted air was like steam.

He ran on till his legs gave out, and when he sank to the ground to have another look at the map, he could hear nothing behind him, human or animal. He got up and plodded on, having almost to hack his way through an overgrown jungle of laurel for several hundred feet. When he got out of that mess, his hands and arms and shoulders, even his face, were covered with sticky residue from the leaves.

Once he was elated at a rumbling sound he thought must be a train, until it came again. Thunder. Still faint and far away to the north. The disappointment drained off the rest of his energy, and he was soon dragging himself forward by sheer will alone. Suddenly, this too was threatened.

Behind him, so close he stopped dead in his tracks, a dog barked. It was so clear he could distinguish a low growl underlying the furious yelping of the beast.

He ran wildly now, breathing raggedly, panting and stumbling and uttering sharp little groans of pain at the stabbing catch in his right side. His scratched and sticky arms lashed aside any branch or bush that stood in his way. There wasn't time to go around them.

Welcome was right. He had talked himself into an act of

madness. When his foot struck a rock half-buried in his path and he sprawled headlong into a shallow gully, he gave up and lay still, waiting to be overtaken. He would fake an injury, pretend to be knocked cold, and he would tell them—he would tell them the dog had scared him into running. Yes, the dog had scared him, and he'd started running and lost his way.

He waited.

His breath eased. His chest relaxed. He had trouble keeping his eyes shut. They flickered open, staring up through tangled branches to a gray sky, thick now as pudding.

Still no one came. No dog barked.

He had a crazy urge to cry out. They must be lurking nearby waiting for him to give himself away with a sound, a movement. He couldn't bear it any longer. He moaned. Nothing happened. He moaned again, louder, and stirred as if in pain and unable to get up. Still they didn't come.

The woods were clammy and darker than dusk. He moaned once more, surely loud enough to be heard by anyone as close as that dog had sounded. As they do before a storm, the birds had become silent.

Not caring what happened, he got to his feet and doggedly trudged onward, not hurrying, not making any effort to be quiet. All he wanted was for the game to end, to be back at the Abbey, to wash the stickiness off his hands and face and the threads of blood off his scratches, to drink a gallon of cold water, to lie down in a cool, dry place.

By now he was paying little heed to anything around him and was only mildly interested in whether he was going in the right direction. Then gradually, as fatigue settled upon him like a heavy but not really uncomfortable coat and there was still no sign of pursuit, he became aware that he had made a long descent into a sparsely wooded valley and was now walking uphill once more through an almost treeless field full of mustard and milkweed.

A grove of poplars jogged his memory.

There was no road. It was not the same area—he was sure of that—but up there ahead—yes! There was even a line of fir trees near the top—it had to be the same ridge. Over that crest must be the ravine and in the ravine—

His legs were running again now and his heart was pumping and the sweat was flowing and the will to reach his goal came surging back stronger than ever.

He made it. He was there. Below him as he topped the ridge, the tracks snaked through the ravine. Before going down the steep bank, he turned and studied the slope behind him and the dark woods beyond. His sharp, young eyes failed to spot any moving object, and there was nothing but silence.

Pride in the accuracy of his calculations raised his spirits and lifted his hopes as he scrambled down the long, steep face of the ravine. Nothing was going to stop him now. And he couldn't have chosen a better spot. A train would have to slow to a crawl around these successive curves. There would be no trick at all in hopping aboard, so long as no one saw him.

A sudden dazzling glimpse of the future came like a burst of sunlight through the clouds. He would be going home a hero, whether anyone knew it or not. He didn't care if anyone ever did know. They would know something had happened; something very important indeed to make such a change in him.

He had escaped a mob of ruffians by racing a train to a crossing; he had lived in a mansion, ridden horses, foiled a plot, kissed a grown woman, hopped a freight.

He danced on the ties, put his ear to the rail, tossed stones into the ditch, and then began walking along the tracks toward Plato Switch. Ahead of him, the tracks curved sharply out of sight. Just before he reached this curve, he looked up at the ridge and saw them.

They loomed against the steely sky like two black birds of prey with outspread wings, poised to swoop.

No place to hide from them; no place to run.

It was their upraised elbows that looked like wings, as they both held binoculars to their eyes, watching him as hawks might watch a rabbit in a ditch.

No sign of a dog. They must have gotten rid of it once they were sure of their quarry's intentions.

He looked hopelessly at the opposite bank. Even if he could scramble to the top, he'd be lost up there; they'd easily track him down.

Nothing to do but run forward, praying a train would come whistling around the bend before they could reach him.

As he ran, he kept glancing up at them, wondering why they didn't move. Then suddenly they weren't there; the long gray sweep of sky was empty.

Still he ran on, leg muscles numb and springless, until soon he was lurching along like a cripple.

A bad mistake. A very bad mistake. Instead of panicking he should have waved up at the men, climbed toward them, stuck to his story of being lost.

Too late now. Maybe a good thing after all. Now there would be an end to all the hocus-pocus; gloves and masks must come off, intentions declared.

No point in torturing himself any longer. Around the bend and he would stop, give up, let them take him. Around the bend—

They were waiting for him.

A gang of them. They stood on the tracks ... but they weren't *stand*ing—yes! They were working!

Section hands!

Maybe the same crew he'd seen the other day, and now they were a sight to gladden his heart even more. A band of angels couldn't have been a sweeter sight to behold.

He would have cried out, but he hadn't the breath left to whisper.

He looked up at the ridge. Still empty. Had they spotted the work crew and given up?

Or gone for help?

One of the workmen saw him now and said something to the others, and they all stopped and stared at him. There were six of them, all enormous, and he hurried toward them without a trace of his natural shyness.

And then he stopped.

He wasn't sure why. It might have been their silence or something he saw on their faces—a curious fierceness—or the way they spread out, as if they were casting a net which they were afraid he would slip through or around.

Maybe they didn't understand. He fought to catch his breath, to be able to speak.

It was when they stopped in front of him that he could feel their hostility. It was something he'd sensed before ... Yes, that first day, the station, the tattooed man, only more intense, the faces of animals or killers.

One of them spoke, a wiry, bearded fellow, slightly older-looking than the others.

"Git over here, boy."

His voice was menacing, and he had cold yellow eyes. Peter didn't like the way he kept rubbing one hand along the handle of his pickax.

Peter didn't move.

"I said git over here, you son of a bitch."

Peter tried to move; he couldn't budge his legs.

The man jerked his head and two of the others stepped forward, grabbed Peter roughly by the arms, and yanked him toward the group.

"Spyin' on us, are ya? Sneaky little bastard!"

"No!" He was appalled by the squeakiness of his voice. "I was running—"

"Where you from, brat?"

"The Abbey. No—I mean, I'm really—"

"He's the one, Hitch!"

This came from a freckled, balding youth with ugly, venomous eyes.

The leader spun his head around. "You sure?"

"Christ, yes! I was in the goddamn truck, wasn't I? We'd a got the bastards if that goddam train hadn't cut us off."

All he had to do was make them understand. An easy matter, if he could only make his heart stop churning and catch a few deep breaths. But the sheer hatred of all those eyes burning into him made him grope and stammer and trip over the words. He could see they didn't believe him, didn't want to believe him. But he could prove it!

"Up there!" He pointed toward the ridge. "They're there. The ones who are after me."

They all looked and saw nothing but the brooding sky.

"Lyin' sonofabitch!" The swarthy one with bull shoulders made a threatening move toward him with a crowbar. The leader pushed him back.

"Hold on there, boys. He ain't gittin' away."

Another one said, "Clete's right, Hitch. Ain't no doubt about it. I was in the truck, too. This is him."

"Hooray!" another one yelled. "We finally got us one o' the bastards."

"What're we gonna do with him, Hitch?"

Now one of the biggest of the men shouldered his way to the front. Black eyes burned in a dead-white face. He grabbed Peter by the hair and jerked his head back.

"Y'all knew my brother. Y'all knew Bart. How he crossed the Ridge durin' deer huntin' last year an' ain't never come back."

"Him an' a lot o' others!" someone cried.

"Well, boys, I aim t' find out here n' now what happened t' Bart. I mean t' find out."

The bearded man made him let go of Peter. "You just wait yer turn, Jess. We got 'im. He ain't gittin' away."

"Make him tell what happened t' Orrie Newton's kid, Hitch. Come back with half his tongue cut out an both hands missin'. Ain't none o' yuh 'd fergit the sight o' that. I seed it. I ain't never gonna fergit."

The white-faced giant licked his lips. "Jesus, there's an idea, Hitch. Do the same damn thing t' this bastard. Cut his goddamn tongue in two."

They all liked this idea. Peter's already parched throat went completely dry. He tried desperately to speak.

" 'Nother word outa you I'm gonna let Jess start carvin'. Got yer knife on ya, Jess?"

The knife flashed.

"Start with his ears!" one of them cried.

They all heard the far-off train whistle. Peter tried to get away, but they were on him like a pack of wolves. A fist sent him reeling against the one called Hitch, who grabbed him by both arms.

"You ain't goin' no place, brat. Ain't no so-called law gonna help y' now. Law says we's nothin' but superstitious hillbillies. Well, maybe we is an' maybe we ain't. We know there's gotta be a reason nobody ain't never gone over the Ridge an' come back less'n he's maimed or mindless."

Again the wail of the train, coming closer.

"Weren't fer the train, we'd o' got 'em last time. Give ya any ideas, Jess?"

"Shit, that'd grind his guts into hash!"

The idea seemed to please them all.

"An' ain't nobody gonna be able t' say it warn't a accident."

"Yeah, but first we's gonna bleed the truth outa the little sonofabitch." The freckled kid was opening his jackknife.

"Time enough. We'll let the noon express have what's left of him."

"Ain't gonna be much if I's got anything t'say about it."

"Hey, boys! Christ, lookit there. He's pissed his pants!"

Peter was beyond caring what happened.

"Git the hell off the fuckin' tracks before we's all ground into dog meat!"

Hitch herded them into the gully, shielding Peter from sight of the train as it rumbled past. As soon as he could be heard, Peter made a last appeal.

"I'm not one of them! My name is Peter Patrick—"

"An' you're bein' chased. They's a long time gittin' here, you lyin' bastard."

"Come on, Hitch. We ain't got all day."

"Then hold onto the runt, damn you."

Two of them pinioned Peter. Hitch had his hands free. He faced Peter.

"Spill it, kid."

"I've told you—please—"

Hitch's open hand spun Peter's head halfway around. His ears rang.

"You's gonna tell me what I wanta know, boy, or there ain't gonna be enough a you hung t'gether fer that train t' tear apart."

"I only know what I've seen at my aunt's and—"

Another blow spun his head the other way.

It made him dizzy; he would have fallen if they hadn't been holding him. As it was, his head dropped forward and he let himself sag heavily in the man's arms. He had to get his breath. He had to make them listen—

"Stand clear o' that boy!"

A voice from outside the group.

No one moved.

"Let him go!"

He fell to the ground.

A man he'd never seen before lifted him to his feet.

A few yards away stood another man holding a rifle. This one he recognized: the caretaker who had warned him that day in the park, the one with the dog.

"Can you walk, boy?"

He took a few wobbly steps.

"Now you fellas better go back to work. We report this to the law, you'd be in a heap o' trouble. Assault with intent to kill."

He raised the rifle, aiming it straight at the leader's belly.

With scarcely a mutter, the crew backed off, picking up their tools and shambling back down the tracks, like animals scared away from a kill by stronger predators.

"You got a short memory, boy. I warned you how easy it is to get lost," the caretaker said with the same unemotional courtesy with which, that other time, he had told Peter to stay closer to the Abbey.

"I was chasing a deer." The lie sprang glibly to his lips. "I didn't know I'd gone so far. And then I did get lost. And then, well . . ."

"Here. We'll help you up the bank."

"I'm okay."

He could have walked all the way back to the Abbey, his bodily fatigue having mysteriously worn off. Tomorrow he would probably feel it, every joint would ache, but right now it was his brain that bothered him; he couldn't seem to think coherently. Something about all this didn't make sense; it had the same elusive, haunting quality of wrongness that had characterized everything that had happened to him. Yet he couldn't pin it down; it was like wearing boxing gloves to catch a butterfly.

"Does Dr. El know?"

"He's been very worried."

"They said people have crossed the Ridge and never come back."

"Stupid hillbillies."

The caretaker reminded him of Krieg, that same cool self-possession, the same air of amused indifference; an almost animal serenity.

When they reached the top of the ridge it began to rain, suddenly and very hard.

They told each other lies and tried to smile as they told them. He was lying and he knew Dr. El and Edward were lying, even though their lies were as persuasive as their smiles. They had to be lying, for now that he'd had time to rest and think back on everything, there were too many things that didn't add up.

Why, for one thing, had the workmen been so unwilling to listen to him?

Even ignorant, superstitious, vindictive hillbillies might have wondered why he should have been running, exhausted and terrified, as they must have seen, along a remote stretch of tracks in the direction of Plato Switch.

It was as if they'd been told what to do. And yet their brutality was all too real—his jaw was still sore.

And why had he been allowed to reach the tracks in the first place? His pursuers must have known he was making a run for it almost as soon as he'd left the park. Evidently they'd been keeping a closer watch on him than he had suspected. And when he'd heard that one lone dog bark not more than a few yards from where he'd been crouching, he knew they must have realized he was practically in their grasp. Yet they had let him go on.

He recalled how docilely that tough bunch of laborers had relinquished their victim and skulked away. True, the caretaker had a rifle and they had only crowbars and pickaxes, but still they might have been expected to show some resistance, even if it had been merely vocal.

In spite of this, he couldn't honestly believe it had all been planned that way. He couldn't believe it was all part of the same plot, that the railroad workers were in cahoots with the Abbey. To believe that would be to believe the narrow escape at the station had also been staged. For what possible purpose? None that was even remotely conceivable.

"What you must understand, cherub," Dr. El had thoughtfully tried to explain, "is that we in the Valley constitute an enclave of prosperity very far removed from the poverty on the other side of the Ridge. Contrary to popular belief, there is nothing ennobling in poverty. That which deprives the body invariably robs the soul as well. It makes men bitter and rancorous. Those poor wretches who assaulted you are the victims of their environment; drudgery has turned them into beasts. Now, drink this and then go to sleep. You'll find it has a most appealing taste."

He dutifully swallowed the syrupy liquid and found that Dr. El was right. It had a rich, fruity flavor which he couldn't place but which had the effect, highly pleasing and unusual, of seeming to lighten every inch of his body. Flesh and bones that had seemed too heavy to move seemed now to float softly on the bed; he could move without effort and seemed, indeed, to drift out of the room—or was it that the room, the house, seemed to drift away from him, as a huge steamship might drift away from a very small and solitary island. His conscious thoughts, like so many babbling passengers, were carried away, leaving him at peace.

A day or so later, just before sunset, Welcome came to his room, looking very pretty with a green satin ribbon in her hair and looking more than ever like a carefree child.

"Well, lovey-dove, after this maybe you'll listen to me."

He looked chagrined. "Did you hear what happened?"

"Of course. It served you right." Then, with a quick, affectionate pinch of his cheek, "But I'm glad you weren't really hurt."

"They wouldn't have hurt me."

Her eyebrows shot up. "That's not the way I heard it, lovey. I heard they were ready to snip your ears off."

Had they told her that to scare her, too? To keep her in line?

"Just part of the act. They were put up to it by Dr. El and Edward."

She gave him one withering look of exasperation. "Peter Patrick, if you're not the most *stubborn*—oh, what's the use? Think what you want. Here's something else you can think about. Miss Celestia's had a stroke."

Somehow it didn't surprise him. "Is she dead?"

"No. Sorry. They didn't murder her, if that's what you're thinking. She can't talk, that's all."

She was studying herself in the mirror, as a child would do, or a woman when she was alone or thought herself unobserved, unpinning the ribbon and holding hairpins in her mouth as she fussed with it, cocking her head from side to side and then repinning it further back. But no, this didn't please her; she put it back where it was, caught Peter watching her in the glass, and made a face at him. Then, as if she'd seen something in his face to interest her, she continued to study it with great seriousness.

"What are you blushing for?"

"'The complexion of virtue.'"

"Does virtue have to frown like that?"

"People do frown when they're worried, you know."

"Poor Peter."

"Poor Welcome," he retorted.

"Oh? What have I done now?"

"It's what they've done to you."

She gave her head a shake, less in vexation than in vanity, appraising the flash of red hair and green ribbon in the mirror. "Now, lovey, so help me, if you start that again—"

"They lie to you. Drug you. Use your body—for ... No one has a right to *use* you."

"Maybe not without permission."

He nearly gasped. "You mean you gave Edward Breed permission?"

"Oh, that's different. Do you like my hair this way?"

"How?"

"With the ribbon—"

"How is that different?"

"He's been nice to me."

He sat down on the bed, keeping his back rigid. "Then it was him."

"I didn't say that."

"I think it was," he said bitterly.

She flounced in front of the mirror. "Suit yourself."

"You were never like this at Aunt Affie's."

She seemed to want to shock him, this time by sticking her belly grotesquely forward. "I suppose you liked me better all puffed up and ugly."

Had any other woman behaved like this he would have been stunned and speechless, but everything about her was more child than woman; it was impossible to be stunned by a child showing off. It was more irritating than anything else.

"You were—nicer then."

Turning soft again, she snuggled down beside him and reached for his hand. "You were different, too."

"No, I wasn't."

"You were a little boy." Her hand slid up his arm. "Now you're like a young man." When he didn't say anything, she took her hand away. "Tell me the truth, lovey. Would you rather be treated like a little boy?"

"Of course not."

"A little boy who likes to make believe that everyone's either a monster or a princess."

"If you mean I make things up, it's not true."

"I'm not saying it's wrong, lovey—for little boys."

"Cut it out, Welcome."

"You get mad like a little boy, too." She jumped to her feet and stood primly before him as if speaking a piece in Sunday school. "Peter's mad and I am glad and I know what to please him, a bottle of ink to make him stink and little Welcome to squeeze him!" The coyness turned raffish; a hoyden glance, a gypsy smile. "I wouldn't scream for help if you squeezed me. I'd like it. I'd like it no matter what you did to me. And I wouldn't want to be drugged." The look turned pensive. "But . . . you don't want to."

At the same time, as if that weren't enough for him to cope with, her fingers started walking across his chest, normally too short a trip, yet somehow she made it seem an endless journey, a vast area, broad as Krieg's chest; and he wondered in the midst of his confusion if it was possible that all girls did not in fact prefer the dark, strong, heroic type, that Welcome actually preferred him to Krieg.

A thing he believed unlikely ever to happen to him, or at least not until some impossibly remote time in the future, now seemed incredibly poised on the brink of reality, could become reality, an experience now and a memory forever, if he were to make a certain move, speak a word, deliver himself up to an emotion which fear still held at bay. He thought of the doors it would open, admitting him to things he'd openly disdained, the companionship of other boys, hearty dim-witted types he'd always affected to scorn.

A grown-up love affair: what a trophy to carry back with him.

And yet he knew he wasn't ready to enter the lists for such a trophy, no matter how dazzling; it hadn't even an honest glamour to it yet, but shone, a distant star in another galaxy. To reach it would mean leaving this present world where there were still too many things he wasn't ready to part with, childish things, no doubt, adolescent fancies, playthings that had little to do with the harsh realities of the everyday world.

"You're frowning again," she whispered. "Your lips are all twisted up tight."

"I'm thinking, that's all."

"Then don't."

She put her arms around him and pressed him to her body, her cheek against his. "Oh, lovey, lovey, we could have such fun this summer."

She moved back, flinging herself down on the bed as if suddenly overwhelmingly tired. "But you'd rather spoil it all, wouldn't you? You're too busy *thinking*." Lying on her back, she pressed her hands over her eyes. "You don't like Welcome. You hate her. You want her to go away and never come near you again."

He couldn't imagine what he'd done to offend her. "I do like you. Very much."

She took her hands away but still didn't look at him. "Then why are you so beastly?"

"I'm not!"

"You are too. You'd rather play this silly game of yours. Sky children! Fairy tales! Why can't you just mind your own business and have fun?"

"You shouldn't talk like this, Welcome."

He wasn't sure whether he ought to feel sorry for her or be afraid of her. The baby, for instance. She did have some awfully funny ideas. Yet she had such a winsome appeal, was so feminine and pretty—the sort of girl you could write poems to or songs about.

"It's the way I feel, lovey." Once more her hand crept out to his. "Besides, we haven't got all year. I'm going away tomorrow. Back to the farm."

He both wanted and didn't want a reprieve. "Then what's the rush? I'm going back to the farm, too."

"Tomorrow?" Her childish directness made him feel immeasurably older.

"Maybe."

"He say you could?"

"Who?"

"Dr. El, of course."

In his richest satirically-adult tone: "What's it matter what *he* says?"

"It does, you know."

"He doesn't own me. If I feel like going, no one's going to stop me." An absurdly terrifying image popped into his head; of being chased through the woods by giant police dogs and being able to run no faster than in a dream.

"Don't bet on it," she said.

"What do you mean?"

"He's the doctor, isn't he? If he says you're to stay, I'm sure Mrs. Juul will agree with him."

Her fingers strayed to his ear and played with it. "If you have to stay here, it won't be much fun for me at the farm."

"Krieg will be there."

"Krieg has other interests."

He was tempted to ask her if she knew about Cleo, but refrained, diverted by the warmly agreeable sensation of being trapped in the magnetic field of another human body, the feeling he'd experienced with Krieg the day they'd gone swimming. Her voice became all at once intensely serious. "Right now I'd do anything, lovey, to prove how much I want you with me."

"Anything?" he dared whisper, knowing it was like giving her the key to a door behind which he could no longer hide.

She gave him a lingering, ardent look. "Anything at all."

He cleared his throat. Her fingers played along his shirt front. "Is the door locked?" she whispered.

"I don't think so."

"You better lock it." When he didn't move, she nudged him. "Go on, lovey. I won't run away."

It was an effort to break free of that strangely magnetic force, but then, having slid off the bed and locked the door, he felt an even stronger resistance to going back.

"Well, don't just stand there, lovey."

Seconds later they were clasped together on the bed. A few kisses and then she pulled away.

"It'll be more fun with our clothes off, lovey."

"We better not."

"Don't be scared."

It had been too long on his mind to scare him; only he wished he'd spent more time in the sun and been more diligent in performing his exercises.

"You might get another baby."

"No danger."

"Why not?"

"Feminine magic."

He giggled, loosening up. "Why didn't you use feminine magic when Mr. Breed—"

"I told you, lovey, that was different."

He wished he could shut his brain off. It would make it all so much easier. It was sure to be a grotesque failure if he tried to do to Welcome what he'd seen Krieg doing to Cleo in the woods. He was too green, too incapable of the savage sort of vitality so plainly evident in their woodland coupling; his brain was too busy, too far ahead of his body, too much in control of the action.

When Welcome got up to close the rust-colored curtains, he wished desperately she wouldn't come back—and just as ardently hoped she would, knowing something terribly important was at stake, something which would shape the destinies of all those Peter Patricks waiting to take possession of their years. And yet the closing of the curtains made the room look sinister, gave an altogether false gravity to the situation, a grimness of purpose which weakened his intentions even further.

Calmly shedding her clothes in the half-light, she looked different, a stranger, a dark lady herself, surely not the girl with the valentine face with whom he'd made rosettes in Aunt Affie's kitchen, and yet he knew *he* was the only *stranger* there, and this lay at the root of his uneasiness. He had no idea how this stranger would or should behave.

He wanted to get up and examine his face in the bureau mirror: would he even recognize it?

"Come on, lovey, I'm way ahead of you."

Naked, she was ever so much prettier to look at than Cleo. Her young body with its firm, round breasts and shapely thighs and buttocks had a soft pearly glow about it in the semi-darkness, as if it generated its own light and heat.

"Here," she said, bending over him, "let me help."

But instead of reaching for the buttons, she snaked a hand around his head and pressed his face between her lustrous breasts and started a sinuous back-and-forth movement, her nipples cruising his lips and cheeks.

All his boyish, vexing, niggling, censuring, wavering doubts crumbled before a bodily urgency as demanding as birth itself.

She repulsed him with a soft, gurgling laugh.

"Promise first, lovey."

"What?"

"No more of *those* games."

He neither knew nor cared what she was talking about.

"I mean it, lovey. No more snooping. No fairy tales. No games. Promise?"

"Yes . . . yes!"

An easy promise, an eager one, for this new Peter Patrick was already ashamed of his connection with the myth-maker, dreamer, boy-child. The quicker he could disown him, the better.

"I promise," he said, unaware of how faithfully he was aping Krieg's blunt, husky, manly tone.

Vast and lasting shifts of fortune might have been accomplished 'thereafter had he not escaped from her embrace and, in a joyful excess of passion, done something the old Peter Patrick would have blushed with shame to think about. His eyes were therefore close enough to see it even in the darkened room.

The star-shaped scar!

His recoil from a poisonous spider would not have been so whip-quick.

"What's wrong, lovey?"

He told her.

"Is that all? I thought you heard something."

"You're one of them!"

What flashed through his brain was one of those wild

surmises that instinct validates above and beyond all colder logic: *they* were the sky children.

"Lovey, you promised. No more games."

"One of the sky children ... you ... Krieg ..."

He was off the bed, tearing open the curtains, as if the scar were indeed a spider which he needed more light to find and kill; but in that flooding sunset glare, the poisonous thing was her face. The sweet valentine had suffered a shocking disfigurement into something ugly and venomous.

More shocking still was her sudden wild shriek of laughter.

"You baby! You baby!" Another ribald eruption of insane mirth; he'd never heard a more horrible sound.

His voice shook. "He sent you here."

She bounced off the bed and snatched on her clothes twice as fast as she had shucked them off.

"You dumb little fag!"

"Dr. El sent you, didn't he?"

"Creep!"

"*Why?*"

She aimed a pestilent glance at him. "You'll find out."

"Welcome!"

"Bye-bye, *lovey*."

She was gone, leaving a trail of laughter that echoed in his brain like the wail of a banshee.

Part Three

Aunt Affie made it clear that from now on Krieg would stick as close to Peter as a sticktight to a possum to make sure he didn't get overfatigued.

"And I," she added, "will see to it you take this lovely tonic Dr. El was so kind to send home with you."

"If that's what it is," he said.

"That's just what it is, and a honey of a one at that. I used to take it myself. So did Luke and Maureen."

"Where are they?" He'd neither seen nor heard the darlings.

"Gone to camp. They asked me to say good-bye to you."

He supposed it was the only way they could be sure Luke wouldn't spill anything he shouldn't.

"Wouldn't it have been simpler if I just went home?"

Gram herself couldn't have looked more innocent.

"Not that I could—without a ticket."

"Ticket?"

"Somebody around here pinched it."

She began to bustle about in that foggy, ineffectual way so characteristic of old ladies and so annoying to young boys.

"I had my return ticket in my bureau drawer. Somebody stole it."

"What nonsense, Peter."

"My diary, too."

She peered at his eye as if it were at the end of a needle and she knew she'd have trouble threading it. "Your *diary?*"

"They stole that, too, but I got it back."

Her dismay might almost have been genuine. "You'd better explain all this, Peter. Less'n you're just tryin' to get my goat."

"It's simple," he said breezily. "I always kept my diary and my return ticket in the small bureau drawer in my

94

room. *Always.* One day I went to get my diary, and it was gone. So was the ticket."

For being feigned, her picture of distress was masterly. "Land sakes, darlin', why didn't you say somethin'?"

"Wouldn't have done any good."

"You makin' all this up to torment me?"

"No! Anyway, the diary came back."

"You musta mislaid it. I'm a great one for doin' that myself."

"Considering it showed up at the Abbey?"

"What about the ticket?"

"Still missing."

Her baffled look amused him, but with it came another feeling, a vain hope that she might be the innocent one among them, the only one he could confide in. She could look so *very* much like Gram. But what did that prove except that she, too, was a monster of duplicity.

"Why on earth would anyone—either here or at the Abbey—want to read a young boy's diary? It don't make sense."

"Maybe they wanted to find out how much I knew."

Her eyes still betrayed nothing but the same depthless innocence. "About what?"

"Things."

"What things?"

"About Welcome's baby, for one thing."

She started, but it was a clap of thunder that took her unawares, the opening salvo of a storm building since early morning. Honeysuckle branches lashed the window. She sketched nervous arabesques across her chest, twiddled her rings.

"Now aren't you glad we took out those light bulbs? What about Welcome's baby?"

"I know all about it, that's all. It's Edward Breed's. They wanted me to believe her baby died and that Edward had a wife. They tried to tell me—"

"Oh, stop, stop, for pity's sake, child. I've never heard such twaddle in all my born days. Now you listen to me, young man. It so happens Welcome is an ignorant, foolish young girl who got herself in a peck of trouble. Dr. El and Mr. Edward helped her out of it. Now as far as you or me or Welcome or anyone else is concerned, that baby of hers is *dead*—"

"But—"

"Now let me finish. Maybe it is and maybe it isn't, but as far as we're concerned, it *is*. Dead and buried. Where Mr. Edward's baby boy came from is likewise none of our beeswax. If it came to bless his loneliness as a result of an act of Christian charity, so much the better. That's all I want to say or hear on the subject. It's not fit for a boy your age. You ought to know that without bein' told."

By the time she finished this speech, her eyes were aglitter with indignation, her chins madly vibrating.

Peter said quietly, "Aunt Affie, why did you want me to come here in the first place?"

She could not have looked more surprised, or more at a loss.

"Why—I'm sorry to confess I didn't—not at first."

"Then what made you change your mind?"

"Your mother—she was—very anxious. I began to feel selfish. And yes, for Abby's sake, I guess. I told you about the rift in the family. I got to thinkin' this might be a way of healin' it, though too late in the day to make any difference really."

An even louder thunderclap exploded directly overhead; a wall of rain leaned against the house. She put her hand on his shoulder. "You're not sorry you came, are you, dear?"

Once again he felt enclosed in the aura of a stronger personality than his own, this time charged not with the remotest sexuality but with a more deeply pervasive warmth, maternal and protective, and he knew he wanted to believe her, wanted all his doubts disproved by love.

"Now then," she declared, taking him firmly by the hand. "What about this wretched ticket? Shall we call the sheriff or shake down the servants ourselves? First off, maybe you and me had best form a posse of two and visit the scene of the crime."

As he let her lead him up the stairs like a child, he marveled at the stillness of the house within the tumult of the storm; it was uncanny, and at each door they passed he fancied an ear pressed to the keyhole listening, listening, listening.

He showed her where he'd kept the diary, without volunteering its present hiding place, and where, in the corner beneath his clean handkerchiefs, he'd kept the ticket, insisting it was a waste of time as she methodically began removing every item from the drawer.

"I know all too well how boys cat-haul things around," she said, not ending her search until she'd removed even the neatly folded, long-yellowed newspaper used to line the drawer. She found nothing but a paper clip and a rhinestone button.

"Satisfied?" he said acidly.

"Not quite." And she proceeded to remove the drawer from its slot, having a rather tricky time dislodging the stops from the rails, then sticking her hand deep into the cavity.

She pulled out the ticket, crumpled but untorn.

"Didn't you think to look back there?"

"Apparently I didn't."

Her eyebrows shot up. "And I know why you didn't. You might have found it, and there'd have been no mystery. Much more fun to think somebody made off with it."

He went red with annoyance. "The diary wasn't back there!"

She put the ticket back where he said he'd kept it. "You can be sure there's an equally simple explanation for that, too."

Doubts compounded with more doubts.

Maybe he was wrong.

As an act of provisional penance, he made no fuss when it was time to take Dr. El's tonic, pleased to discover it had a most agreeable raspberry flavor, and suspecting with interest that there was more than a dollop of alcohol in it: perhaps Dr. El's revenge was to send him home a precocious and incurable alcoholic. If so, he was ready to cooperate, even venturing to search Aunt Affie's room one afternoon in hopes of enjoying an illicit snort.

He didn't find it.

Dog days and the tranquilizing effect of Dr. El's tonic sapped his energy, leaving him content to spend most of his time dabbling with his watercolors or curled up on the porch swing with a book, or napping in his room.

The house continued to have that curiously deserted air he'd first noticed the night of the storm.

He accepted everything they told him and believed nothing.

He accepted the sensation of gentle drifting.

They're waiting for you to go.

He very nearly said it out loud, a thought from nowhere, but extraordinarily vivid.

Pursuing it, he asked himself who was waiting for him to go.

Cleo?

Yes! And maybe others. Maybe all of them.

Across the pond from him, Krieg was studiously making some small repair to the dory's hull; with his gift for total involvement he might have been thinking of nothing else; Peter was sure he wasn't.

He was sure, also, that Krieg wasn't waiting for him to go, or if he was, he didn't care how soon; it would be all the same to him, and Peter both envied and despised him for this maddening impartiality.

Welcome was the same way. What you thought was enthusiasm could just as well have been indifference.

The sky children were all like that, he supposed. He still believed that those star-shaped scars were emblems of the sky children, and if he knew *who* they were, or who some of them were, he still didn't know what they were.

Thinking about it, he liked to imagine them as a secret society, a cult, engaged in various dark rites, meeting by moonlight somewhere in the wildest part of the Brokenstraw forest, performing curious, obscene rituals, sacrificing to lusty pagan gods, dancing to the pipes of some bucolic Pan.

In truth, he feared it was much duller and more innocent, perhaps occasional square dances in the grange hall for these hired hands and winsome milkmaids who took the same ingenuous delight in their secret brands as Masons did in their clandestine symbols. What they truly had in common was perhaps nothing more praiseworthy than a certain rustic wantonness in their erotic lives, being either willing victims of their lusts like Locky, or victimizers, as Welcome had tried to victimize him and as Krieg had victimized Cleo Juul.

Poor Cleo. Peter had only to look at her when Krieg was present to see how deeply she was still infatuated. Those secret, longing glances she would flash at Krieg, seldom at his face and never eye to eye, but at the fringes of his physical being, as it were, at foot, hand, hip, shoulder, then quickly away, as if to look at him only fed the desire which nothing but a touch would satisfy. Peter would observe the grinding movement of her fingers, the rubbings and clenchings, the spastic nervous gestures, and the frustration which fed upon itself in her craving eyes.

That she resented Peter he had no doubt whatsoever.

Sometimes, feeling himself the cause of her distempered silence, he would have liked to tell her it was not his idea that Krieg spend so much time with him, and that he could hardly be held responsible for any falling away of Krieg's affection. In fact, he might have tried to convey this message, if only by innuendo, had he not learned to distrust even his strongest convictions. Much of this byplay between Krieg and Cleo might be all in his imagination.

But then he discovered it was not.

Cleo had surprised him one morning at the breakfast table by her unwonted cheerfulness, the hectic gaiety of a suddenly cured invalid.

A short time later, he asked Krieg if he should have their horses saddled for the usual morning ride.

Krieg looked thoughtful. "Maybe later, sport. I've got to take Mrs. Juul into town."

"Aunt Affie?"

"Nope. The other one."

His tone was not flattering to Cleo, and yet Peter felt a twinge of jealousy at the thought of Krieg and Cleo driving the long, twisting roads into Brokenstraw, perhaps stopping in some secluded spot and leaving the car and stealing off among the trees and stripping themselves naked and again performing that savage act upon a bed of leaves and pine needles.

So that when Krieg said, "Come along with us, why don't you, sport," Peter was quick to agree. Then he hesitated.

"You sure you want me to?"

"Well, I do see more than enough of you now, that's true." He paused, grinned. "You been awful mopey since you got back from the Abbey. Trip to town might put some life in you."

"I'll tell Aunt Affie."

There was an odd gleam in Krieg's bright eyes. "No call to do that, sport."

"She'll wonder where I am."

"You'll be with me—that's all that matters. I'm supposed to keep an eye on you, and I can't do that if I'm in town and you're horsin' around out here."

Why should he care if Aunt Affie knew? Was there

something fishy about it? And Peter suddenly got that tight, excited feeling in his chest which he always got when he thought he'd finally got Krieg at a disadvantage.

"I still think I better let her know."

In an ugly man, Krieg's look would have been murderous. "You tell her," he said, deadly calm, "an' you ain't likely to go."

"Why not?"

"Just take my word for it."

Baiting the beast of anger that never quite got past Krieg's defenses, Peter said, "You know Aunt Affie's rules."

"Then skip it, sport." He started to turn away.

"You're the one asked me to go."

"Sorry I did."

"Okay, Krieg. I won't say anything."

Krieg's glance was suddenly warm. Peter was surprised. Krieg really wanted him to go.

When Cleo saw Peter in the car, her face, naked with outrage, told Peter the whole story.

"What are you doing here?"

Peter didn't move. "I'm going with you."

She looked at Krieg.

"Is he?"

More than her tone, it was the looks between the two that confirmed Peter's suspicions. In Cleo's gauntlet-casting defiance were revealed months of subterranean lovers' warfare, endless skirmishes of glance and innuendo, nights of sleepless longing, and more than anything else, a souring sexual rapport, still vital at her end, jaded and fatigued at his.

"He is." Krieg's tone was mild but firm.

For several seconds, he made no move to open the door for her, which Peter interpreted as a challenge to her to break the date, change her mind, fling herself around and march back to the house; and this, were she to do it, would signal the end of the affair, Cleo's surrender.

She stood her ground, thin, pale lips quivering at the corners.

Krieg, blank-faced, came around and opened the door for her, and Cleo climbed into the car and huddled as if cold in the back seat behind Peter.

The atmosphere remained chilly until, halfway to town, Krieg suddenly broke into song.

"Old Bumpy is daid and laid in his grave, ohhh, ohhh, ohhh..."

It was a funny, rollicking, bawdy song; Peter couldn't help laughing, although he was genuinely shocked and knew that his laughter was as pointedly cruel as the song.

One afternoon shortly after this, when Peter and Krieg were out riding, a sudden late-summer storm blew gusts of rain in sheets over the mountain, flooding the eastern slope of the Ridge and drenching them to the skin. The pounding rain and ear-cracking thunder drove Peter into hysterics, there was something so witlessly comic in urging their mounts along the trail when they themselves were already as wet as it was possible to be. It seemed madness to him that Krieg should lead them deeper into the hills instead of back toward the farm.

There was a reason. They came eventually to a cabin in a clearing; Krieg hitched the horses under an attached lean-to.

"Welcome to the Old Log Inn, sport." He grinned wickedly. "There's a joke goes with that, but never mind. Will you cut out that giggling!"

"I c-c-can't, Krieg."

Krieg shut the door behind them, grabbed him by the shoulders, and gave him such a shaking he couldn't tell his teeth from his toes. He stopped giggling and looked around. A rough stone fireplace across one wall, with enough stacked firewood for a Siberian winter. Nothing else, not even a chair or table, nothing but a stained gray-and-white-striped mattress and a kerosene lantern hanging from a nail on the log wall.

Krieg set about making a fire while Peter, shivering violently, listened to the clatter of the rain on the corrugated roof. When Krieg had a good fire blazing he turned to Peter, unsmiling even though Peter knew what a comical sight he must be with his hair plastered to his head and water dripping off his nose and chin. He looked around, hoping there might be at least one blanket.

"Sport, your auntie's gonna nail my hide to the barn door for this."

"It's not y-your f-f-fault, Krieg." He'd end up with a filthy cold, at the very least. Soon, however, the fire began doing its job, the first thick waves of heat licking out at them, the water from Peter's hair sizzling on the hot logs.

"You're gonna put the damn fire out!"

Krieg gave him a grim look, crossed the room, and dragged the soiled mattress back in front of the fire, then peeled off his sopping shirt and pants and shorts and told Peter to do the same.

Draping them over the stone mantel, he told Peter to lie down.

Peter knelt on the mattress, facing the flames.

"I said *down*, cuss your hide!"

Peter giggled once more, pretending to flinch. "What are you going to do, Krieg?"

"Keep you from getting a snotty nose, with any luck." And with this he pulled Peter to him as he stretched out on the mattress. Peter made no fuss; it was the way animals kept warm, and with the fire's heat on his bare back and the warmth of Krieg's body in front, he was soon back to normal, and though he still shivered it was because Krieg's big rough hands kept rubbing up and down his back.

"How come your hands are so rough?" he asked him, and Krieg laughed and said, "Yours'd be, too, if you ever did a lick o' work with 'em."

"When do you ever work so hard?"

"You think I spend all my time playin' nursemaid?"

Peter's face was hard against Krieg's satiny brown shoulder. "Not all your time, I *know* that."

"Oh?"

But this wasn't quite the time for spilling what he knew about Krieg's amorous exploits: the very roughness of those hands intimidated him.

"Well," he answered, backing down, "I assume you must have some other kind of work—besides unscrewing light bulbs for Aunt Affie."

"I'm a woodsman, sport. I know every trail and tree in these parts. Been a mill hand, sawyer, every job you can name had anything to do with lumber."

"Then tell me what kind of wood this floor's made of."

"Easy. Tree wood." He reached up and pushed Peter's face into the mattress, and then they were wrestling and Peter thought of Krieg and Cleo in the woods and of Locky tethered to the stable walls, screaming under the lash and yet somehow marvelously, rawly alive. Alive! And of Theron with his long, booted legs spread wide and his hands engaged in—an act of life!

It was a glimpse of something in the darkness of his

nature, something deep below the surface of his brighter dreams and nobler fantasies, something irreconcilable with them, but unmistakably *there* in his warm bones and young body and brimming flesh, and it was like the darkened room at the Abbey on the bed with Welcome ...

The sky children's game. And he was part of it—could be part of it—wanted to be part of it. And yet—

"Welcome's got a scar like yours. So has Locky."

Their playful scuffling ceased. Peter heard the silence outside and knew the rain had stopped.

Krieg was on his back, not so much as a hair on his arm touching Peter.

"You want to know how I found out, Krieg? About Welcome?"

"You're a snoop."

"You don't want to know when I saw it?"

"Nope."

And he didn't! He honestly didn't.

"It means she's one of the sky children, doesn't it?"

Krieg didn't answer.

"Well, doesn't it?"

"Get your duds on, sport."

"Not till you tell me."

"Rain's stopped. We can start back."

"Are they—bastards, Krieg?"

The notion had come to him that morning as he lay in bed thinking about Welcome's baby, and he had wondered ...

"The sky children—are they—bastards? Love children. You know. And then they're branded so everyone will know what they are. And they can't get decent jobs. They have to be servants. And nobody cares what they do—I mean, morally ..."

He felt himself losing control, drifting dangerously close to tears. "I wanted to help you. Maybe I was wrong about everything, but I still wanted to help. You, and Welcome, too. Both of you. I liked you and wanted to help you. I thought you loved each other. I wanted—I wanted—"

He couldn't go on, didn't know what he was saying, stumbled over the words that didn't begin to say what he felt inside, what it was he wanted, had always wanted, and had seemed so close to—touching ...

"Ease off, sport. You're tuckered out—"

"Quit babying me, you—you bastard!"

"Sport—"

"You could have helped me. The rest of them won't. I hate them all. But you—you—"

"Sport, it don't concern you."

"It does! I want—"

"You want to be part of it. That it?"

Yes, yes! Part of it. The mystery, the brightest of mysteries—and the darkest.

"Please let me, Krieg. Please let me."

Krieg sadly shook his head; the fire had dried his hair and curled it into ringlets, a fit crown for a pagan god.

"You'll be goin' home, sport."

"But I've got to *know*, Krieg."

Krieg laughed. "That I'm a bastard?"

"I didn't mean that."

"Thanks."

"Then what, Krieg? What? I swear to God I won't tell."

"We gotta hightail it outa here before it lets loose again. Now get a move on."

Peter stared sulkily into the fire. "I know somebody who'll tell me."

"Who's that, sport?"

"None of your business."

He was only bluffing, and Krieg probably knew it, but the older man's mocking laughter stung him. By the time they got back to Sugar Hill, he had made up his mind what to do.

Taking Luke's bike was easy. He stole out after dark and wheeled it to the bottom of the lane, where he hid it in the underbrush near the road, and after breakfast next morning, when the coast was clear, he packed a few sandwiches and was on his way.

Pedaling through the woods between Sugar Hill and the Abbey, he thought of a certain engraving in his copy of *Idylls of the King* showing a solitary knight on horseback crossing a romantic bosky glen and seeing far-off and immaterially bright upon a distant peak the castle to which he is traveling, bathed in the light of a poet's moon. This morning the sun was shining. He was no knight, and this three-speed job of Luke's was not exactly a pacing steed; yet he couldn't possibly have felt more adventurous.

About a half mile from the Abbey he hid the bike in a clump of poison sumac high on the creek bank but not too near the road and carried his sandwiches down to the water's edge where he couldn't be seen. All that pedaling and the nervous excitement of what he planned to do had quickened his appetite. He sat watching dragonflies shimmering over the creek, all aglitter in the noon sun.

Finishing this meager lunch, he climbed back to the road, made some vague calculations with the aid of his pocket compass, and having satisfied himself that he knew where he was going, left the bike where it was hidden and struck off through the woods at an angle which he felt confident would bring him close to the eastern border of the Abbey gardens, the part where Miss Celestia had habitually been left alone for a short midafternoon airing.

Hardly a prayer that the habit was still practiced, but this was the only way to find out.

As it happened, his calculations were slightly inaccurate, having led him to a point a quarter of a mile short of the mark, and he had to skirt the edge of the park, keeping an eye peeled for the caretaker and his dog, until he came to the Abbey itself, whereupon he ducked back into the woods, made a wide semicircle, and came at last to the garden wall near the spot where he was hopeful of finding Miss Celestia.

Climbing the wall was a cinch; avoiding the eye of the gardeners was the tricky part. He clung to the top of the wall long enough to spot one of the gardeners less than a hundred feet beyond the wall, but fortunately his back was turned, he was alone, and he was using electric hedge clippers which would not only require all his attention, but would effectually deafen him should Miss Celestia cry out.

To Peter's surprise the old lady was in fact there, lying peacefully on a chaise longue in the shade of a clematis-draped trellis, to all appearances fast asleep, and, for the moment, unguarded.

Peter dropped to the ground, faced with the truth that he hadn't really expected Miss Celestia to be there—not when he'd plotted his adventure, not when he was pedaling toward the Abbey, not when he was eating his lunch, and not when he'd climbed the wall. It was the flight he'd wanted—the joy and excitement of escape.

Now it had become truly an adventure of epic proportions. Real danger must be faced if he was to go through with it. *Non ignara mali* and all that.

There was no time to be tricky about it. No telling how soon Weems would be back to fetch Miss Celestia.

Again he climbed the wall, paused once more to be sure he was unobserved, and dropped lightly to the ground. He saw at once that Miss Celestia was not asleep but was watching him, betraying her excitement only in the flash and glitter of those magnificent eyes. Nevertheless, he pressed a finger to his lips as he hurried forward and crouched at her side, grateful for the protection of the trellis behind him, although the gardener with the shears was in front of them and had only to turn around to see them.

Speaking rapidly, he told her why he was there, spilled out his fragmentary clues about the sky children.

Tears welled up in the corners of her eyes; her lips, oddly twisted, tried vainly to frame words.

Hopelessly, he realized Welcome had told him the truth. The old lady was indeed speechless.

He pressed her hand and leaned closer. "I'm sorry. But you do hear me, don't you?"

Her head moved up and down.

"You tried to tell me about the sky children, didn't you?"

Once more a nod.

"I've tried my best to find out more. No one will tell me anything."

Her facial response was unmistakable.

"Is it dangerous for me to know?"

A quick nod.

His eyes kept track of the gardener, who, in another few moments, would have moved out of sight behind a huge magnolia bush. Good.

Before he could ask another question, Miss Celestia pointed shakily toward the house.

"You're afraid Weems will come back?"

Nodding, she worked her fingers as if she were writing.

"You want to write it down. I'm sorry—I don't have anything to write—"

Her head made a swift, impatient negative sign. He looked puzzled. Once more she made scribbling movements, then pointed toward the house. Surely she couldn't want him to run to the house and find paper and pencil!

For an instant she, too, seemed to panic, swayed her body in a torment of anguish, rubbed her hands together, then abruptly grabbed his arm and shook it and then pointed to herself and once again pretended to write, paused, made a backward waving gesture.

A smile burst over his face. "You *have* written it down! You already have."

A deep, satisfied, weary nod.

"Where?" he asked urgently, an eye on the magnolia bush.

This time it was simple. She made as if to open a book and read its pages.

"In a book?"

Yes.

"You've written it down and it's in a book."

Her hands closed the invisible volume, turned it, indicated the spine by pulling him closer and touching his own backbone.

"Yes! Yes! I understand. Now where is the book?"

Again at the house and then at herself.

"In your room?"

Yes.

"The name of the book."

She pointed at him.

"Me?"

She jabbed her finger at him again more emphatically.

"Me? I?"

He despised his own stupidity, and hoped Miss Celestia wouldn't have another stroke on the spot. At the same time he could almost feel the indomitable Weems threading her way among the flower beds with Miss Celestia's wheelchair.

Desperately, he said, "I'm sorry . . . I'm sorry . . ."

Suddenly she pointed at herself instead.

"You?"

Her eyes burned brighter. She pointed eagerly at her rings.

"Ring?"

No, no.

"Rings?"

A sharp, exasperated shake of her head. This grim game of charades was wearing them both down. Peter searched her eyes for telepathic help. She pinched the elaborate old-fashioned setting and wiggled it back and forth on her finger.

"Diamond!"

A grateful nod.

"Your diamond—"
No.
"Your—"
No, no, no.
"You!"
Yes.
"You diamond—"
Almost.
"You diamonds . . ."
You diamonds. You diamonds . . .
Her eyes burned encouragement.
"You . . . *Eustace Diamonds?*"
Right!

Trollope's *Eustace Diamonds*, the novel for which she'd said she had such a special fondness.

"*Inside* the *Eustace Diamonds.*"

The spine. Inside the spine.

Her face all at once went rigid. Her body gave a violent jerk.

Weems!

In a split second he was behind the trellis, screened from Weems's view but in full sight of the gardener, who had shut off the clippers and appeared to be making some adjustment to them. Weems didn't say a word as she hoisted her charge onto the wheelchair and started back toward the house.

There was no time for caution. He darted to the wall and clambered over. As soon as his feet touched the ground, he sprinted through the trees toward the Abbey. He heard no one behind him.

He knew there was more danger, once he had to come out of the woods again and cross to the house, in being furtive than in being forthright. At the margin of the lawn, he paused only long enough to make sure there was no one in sight at that moment, then he walked swiftly but casually out of the woods and toward the house quite as if he were there on a normal visit.

No one challenged him, and yet he felt that every window was occupied by curious, unfriendly eyes, set to trap him once he'd been fool enough to enter the house itself.

He slipped into the hall and waited.

Footsteps along the passage into the gallery above.

He darted forward, twisted the banister and scurried

into the secret chamber. He was Charles Stuart himself now, in bedraggled but nonetheless royal satin and lace.

Footsteps down the stairs, across the hall. A door opened and shut. He waited a few seconds before opening the small door and stepping out.

He sped up the stairs, watched only—he hoped—by the painted eyes of ancient Breeds.

It was too easy.

The house might have been deserted, not a voice, not so much as a whisper; silence like this in so big a house was uncanny.

He paused outside Miss Celestia's door, the thought bringing him up short: could it all be a trap?

Even Miss Celestia?

Why would she, the matriarch of the house of Breed, try to subvert her own nephews by confiding secrets to a stranger, a boy, someone she scarcely knew?

Intuition's warnings are as obscure as destiny's pattern.

His eyes knifed through the gloom for signs of ambush in the dim passage. Or were they in Miss Celestia's room, behind the door, ready to pounce the instant he crossed the threshold? In his mind he saw Dr. El's face, not the glabrous pussycat smile, so archly seductive, but the devil's mask it had worn up there on the ridge above the burying ground—my God, he could almost hear him breathing behind the door—and could see his narrow white hand tensed around a poison-glutted needle.

Peter shivered, imagining the sting of the deadly hypo. The air hung heavy with death and silence ...

A muted jangle of distant cowbells broke the spell; from somewhere in the woods a dog barked. The caretaker's German shepherd?

He opened the door and slipped into the boudoir of Miss Celestia's suite. The air reeked of medicines. Hurrying to the window, he peeped through the heavy tussore silk curtains in time to see Miss Celestia being wheeled across the terrace, some long-stemmed white roses in her lap, no doubt the only delaying tactic she'd been able to manage. Bless her for that.

Luckily, he found the book at once, lying in plain sight on the marquetry table beside the bed.

He snatched it up and extracted from the spine beneath the binding a tightly folded manuscript written on thin leaves of tissue paper.

Not taking time to unfold it, he slipped it into his shoe and made his escape, scarcely caring if he was intercepted now as he stole along the passage toward the stairs, feeling indeed very breezy and daredevilish, anticipating an encounter and having the words ready on his lips.

"But where is everybody?" he would say. "I've just cycled over from the farm. My bike broke down and I had to leave it . . ."

Yes, he honestly wished he'd run into one of them; the epic nature of this adventure demanded hardships, meetings with the enemy, narrow squeaks.

He would like to outfox Dr. El face to face.

But not a soul appeared as he tripped down the stairs, across the hall, and out into the sunshine, with such absurd ease he could not help wondering again if something was wrong. Glancing back, he thought he saw a face high in a window of the east wing: a pale, thin face—Dr. El's? He paused, shading his eyes; the sun glimmered on the pane; it might not have been a face at all. Nevertheless, he turned, dropped his nonchalant pose, and streaked into the woods.

He didn't consider himself safe until he'd reached the bank where he'd hidden the bike and made sure it was still there. Incredibly, for hours seemed to have passed, it was still early afternoon—how quickly it had all happened. Only a few cobblestone clouds bridged the sky. There was more than enough time to reach the farm before sundown, and though he'd relished the thought of reading Miss Celestia's manuscript in the snug safety of his own room, its appeal to his curiosity was too strong. Those mysterious cramped pages of script were burning a hole in his sock.

And so, with breathless interest, he burrowed down into that green nest, once more scanned creek and woods and bank above him to make sure he was alone, removed the papers from his shoe, admired for a second the elegant symmetry of the handwriting with its fancy, old-fashioned loops and whorls, and then began reading Celestia Breed's story.

Part Four

"The voices came to me, Celestia Breed, first in the garden in the midst of a thundercloud, and like that Hound of Heaven have pursued me constantly, night and day, beseeching me to be the handmaid of the Master who is Jesus Christ and to expose this wickedness of which my forebears were the authors and my nearest blood kin the perpetuators. Reader, I implore your trust.

In this green valley has my family prospered, not from the sweat of their bodies and the purity of their souls, but by darker means, the evil shadows of which still stretch from ridge to river and which have made me, even in this day and age, a virtual prisoner in my own house, where I have penned this indictment at the urging of His Angels in hopes that someone shall learn of this abomination and be the instrument of its abolition.

Abomination. I use the word deliberately, knowing it is a verbal brickbat beloved of anarchists and precious to fanatics, for I speak of an evil that is truly hellish. Lest my words be dismissed as the ravings of a lunatic, let me freely confess that for more than a score of my adult years I was blind to the viciousness of this evil, having been reared under this system as a child, believing it to be universal, proper, moral, and natural.

Even now I am not wholly convinced I am right and they are wrong. I know only that I love Jesus Christ and shall not thwart His will as delivered to me by His Holy Angels whose trumpets have sounded in the flowers and whose voices have come to me out of the clouds. I must obey the will of my Lord. God is my Master and I shall obey Him.

If I appear to dodge, to equivocate, to ramble, it is because I desire perfect understanding. If I shout, it is because I know the deafness of skeptics.

Ethics is a world of shades and shadows. How can I condemn as totally reprehensible a system that has created, as I can see from the window beside which I write, a veritable paradise? The beauty of the countryside is everywhere visible. The sky is pure, the earth is clean. Here is literally a land of milk and honey, where people 'live and lie reclined on the hills like gods together, careless of mankind.' A lotus land.

What then is so abominable about such a condition? I cannot say. I know only that God is angry. I do not question God's wrath. He is my Beloved Master. I obey Him in all things. I alone cannot decide what is right and what is wrong. In many ways Life has never really touched me. My judgments as a thinking individual must come from literature and from a narrow and limited view of the world. Not, assuredly, from conscience alone do I speak, for I do not believe in the independent, autonomous conscience, that sterile godless handmaid of the superego. Conscience is always socially conditioned, and therefore suspect. The soul is not.

It may be that I have spent too much time in my father's library. Indeed, I've read my way through them all: the questers and the jesters, the crabby dogmatists, the idealists and the ideologists, the canting preachers and the subtle persuaders, and I have 'come out by the same door as in I went.'

But perhaps it would be wiser, lest you fear being drawn into an endless fuzzy web of ill-spun dialectics, to forgo the argument till later and present the facts. So be it.

I do not remember my mother, nor have I ever seen a picture of her. I had a brother named Adam, my father's heir apparent, who had a wife, Tirzah, and two sons, Edward and Eldred. Adam and Tirzah both died during an influenza epidemic, in their early twenties. I was responsible for rearing their two boys, but since my own father was a man of forceful character and physical endurance and lived till the boys were of man's estate, my influence was negligible;

they were formed by his stronger hand. When I was instructed by the Holy Voices in the error of our ways, it was too late to redirect their sympathies. The mold had hardened. My childhood was so happy I might have been the daughter of a king, and nothing clouded that happiness until a certain day when I witnessed by chance something I did not understand but which planted the seed of distress which eventually was lightened by the saving grace of my Master. In the old days a sawmill and a complex of farm buildings stood where you now see gardens and terraces worthy of a Nebuchadnezzar. At the time of which I speak, these buildings were little more than relics, and my father was already planning to raze them and replace them with the present horticultural wonders. I must have been eleven or twelve on that evening when I wandered into the barn in pursuit of my kitten, Angelica. I had been tucked in for the night and the housekeeper, Mrs. Bledsoe, would have been upset had she known I had climbed from my room down the catalpa tree to retrieve this errant feline. My father would have been furious.

The hapless creature had somehow got up into the loft, and I had no choice but to follow, tucking my nightdress around me as I scaled the narrow vertical ladder. Having captured the naughty truant, I was about to climb down when the barn door opened, and I shrank back, fearful of discovery. Of course, I assumed that whoever had come in would go about his business and leave. Luckily, Angelica curled up in the straw and went to sleep, for the man who entered the barn showed no signs of leaving, busying himself at some task I could not identify, hearing only an occasional clank of metal.

It being autumn, dusk was no more than a fleeting shadow in the van of night, so that I was soon trapped not only in the loft but in a gloom so deep I could easily imagine bats and mice surrounding me, readying the most bloody assaults. Still the man did not go, and while I was trying to work up the nerve to declare my presence and accept my punishment, the door opened once more, and I heard others come in. Lanterns were lighted, for which I was in one sense relieved, even though they cast the most terrible shadows upon the rafters above me. I lay perfectly still, pretending to be asleep should anyone venture into the loft.

I could hear four distinct voices, one of which was my father's—no mistaking that ponderous trumpet of authority. Another was that of Mr. Lipscomb, our foreman, and the other two belonged to trusted farmhands. From snatches of conversation that floated up to me, it soon became clear that they were awaiting the arrival of someone else, for every few minutes my father could be heard opening the door, spitting into the night and cursing someone's tardiness. Meanwhile, the occasional clanking noise could still be heard, and presently I became aware of something burning. The night was warm, and I could not imagine why they should light a fire. Then it occurred to me that one of the farmhands was also the blacksmith. An odd time and place for such activity, I thought. Alarmed lest the smoke set me to coughing, I covered my mouth with a handkerchief and prayed Angelica would not awaken and betray our presence.

I could easily have ended my anxiety and my acute physical discomfort by crawling out of the loft and confessing I'd fallen asleep up there after chasing Angelica. Although a stern disciplinarian, my father was not a tyrant, and my punishment would have been more likely fair than drastic. I can only say that some whispery sense of iniquity was communicated to me by the furtiveness of speech and movement in that gathering below me, a dim awareness of something irregular, something I should have been severely condemned for witnessing, and this feeling grew stronger as midnight came and went; by then I had abandoned any hope that Mrs. Bledsoe might check my room, find I was gone, and raise a hue and cry that would result in my discovery, apparently sound asleep, in the loft. Indeed, I may have dozed off, for I remember giving a start at the sound of wagon wheels and horses' hooves in the farmyard, and I heard my father cry out, 'Here at last! Look sharp, you men!'

The door opened and strange voices were added to those I knew. It sounded as if supplies were being unloaded, but it was not until I heard a soft, bleating cry, and someone sobbing, that I knew the supplies were human.

One of the men murmured something and presently the blubbering stopped; by then I was in a perfect frenzy of terror and listened with pounding heart as the human cargo was unloaded and carried to a remote end of the barn, after which, I devoutly prayed, the men would disperse and I could find my way back to my own room.

Instead, the horror had only begun.

There was further subdued talk among the men, and then I heard two of them wander away and return amidst sounds of scuffling and childish cries of protest, interspersed with rude laughter and obscene jokes from the men. This was followed by the sound of hands gently slapping at naked skin and a scream quickly gagged into a moan. Again a clank of metal, followed by the most dreadful sound of all: the sizzle of hot metal upon flesh.

A sort of wild, choking, animal sound, and then a curious deep silence followed by the sound of a body being dragged back into the barn's interior.

This almost identical succession of sounds, and the even more frightful images they conveyed to my mind, were repeated six or seven times. Sometimes, beguiled perhaps by the comeliness of one of the victims, or provoked to lustful frenzy by the sight of young, struggling naked flesh, the men would interrupt their grim business and words and sounds would drift up to me which were all the more hideous because I could only dimly apprehend the actions they must have accompanied. Indeed, it was all a nightmare in which my mind, having known only pleasure and peace, could make no connection between the sounds overheard and aught that I had ever experienced. It did not end until the children or youths—they couldn't have been much older than I—were once again loaded into the wagon and taken away, whereupon my father and the other men left the barn and I was alone in the blackness of a stygian cave, clutching Angelica to my breast and forcing myself to wait several minutes before carefully feeling my way down out of the loft, out of the barn, across the dew-soaked grass, and up the catalpa tree into my own dear room.

Miraculously, the cloud passed; its shadow lingered. Though I knew it had been real, I forced myself to think of the experience as a nightmare, sometimes half convincing myself it was. I did not allow myself to reflect on what it all might have meant until about two years later, when something happened that I could not help relating to what I'd heard that night in the barn.

I have alluded to the housekeeper, Mrs. Bledsoe, a dear, simple creature, a surrogate mother, but one who carefully prevented my becoming too deeply attached to her, being warmhearted, kind, and attentive, yet only circumspectly affectionate; a large, handsome woman who seemed as durable as oak until a certain day when I was fretting because my tea was late and had finally to go and look for her. My brother was away at school and Father off on a business trip. Not finding her in the kitchen or pantry, I at length went up to her room and knocked on the door, through which I thought I could hear a faint groaning. When I got no answer I opened the door and saw Mrs. Bledsoe lying naked except for her shift on the floor beside the bed. By the time I reached her, the profoundly silent look upon her face told me she was dead.

The seizure had evidently occurred suddenly and she had fallen to the floor in such a way that her shift was pulled up above her waist, and I noticed upon her thigh the clear whitish impression of a star.

I thought it very curious but attributed no undue significance to it until some time after the shock of her death and the emotional stress of her loss had subsided, and then my mind made a connection for some reason between that odd scar and what had happened that night in the barn, for how else, I wondered, could so perfect an impression have been made except by a branding iron.

In my innocence, which I had no reason to believe my brother did not share, I mentioned the scar to Adam, whose interest in medicine, a somewhat morbid one I thought (and which he seems to have bequeathed to his son Eldred), was already strongly pronounced. His reaction to my comments surprised me by its evasiveness, and I was led to suspect he had access to some secret from which I had been barred. Recklessly, I made additional vague but suggestive remarks and was gratified to observe how very distraught he became, and knowing what a tattletale he was, I was not too surprised to be summoned into my father's presence the following morning, where I was filled at first with apprehension by his long, cold appraisal of me as I stood before him. His manner was judicial, mine felonious.

After sizing me up in this way and seeming to have found the results distasteful, he said: 'Your brother informs me you've been displaying a most unwholesome and unladylike curiosity about matters that do not concern you. Is this true, my pet?'
'They must concern me, Father,' I answered boldly.
'And why must they, pray?'
'If they did not, I would not be here, would I?'
This answer seemed to amuse him; he smiled and told me to sit down.
'I suppose it is high time your education in certain matters was undertaken,' he said, and thereupon began a lengthy and often shocking discourse which left me alternately hot and cold, which sometimes set my heart to beating wildly and sometimes quite froze my blood.

He spoke of pride, of the *hubris* of the Breeds which would not allow them to tolerate the decline of the family fortunes. To farm their vast lands and to mill the lumber from the forests required an abundance of labor, and in the age of legal slavery they had not the means to purchase this commodity. They solved the problem by raiding farms and settlements on the other side of the Brokenstraw Range and stealing youths from their homes, offspring of the poverty-stricken, youths accustomed to little more than a brutish existence.

These youths were branded with a star and put to work in the fields and forests, not as slaves—this was a forbidden word—but as 'sky children,' wards of destiny, who were made to work and work hard, but never to the point of exhaustion, as had been their lot; indeed, they were allowed to rest as often as they were forced to work. They were well fed and suitably sheltered. They were encouraged to breed, and their offspring were distributed among the other farms, all established by branches of the Breed family. Compared with the rigorous lives they had been used to, this was freedom.

The population of the sky children had to be controlled, of course. The boys were all vasectomized at fifteen—my father spared me nothing once he'd decided the time had come for my enlightenment—and could therefore enjoy all the pleasures of sexual congress with no fear of impregnating any of their partners. In other words, the sky children enjoyed all that their masters enjoyed, and in addition were freed of all material and moral responsibilities. Perhaps as a result of this, they were generally docile, temperate, and handsome, strong of body and cheerful in disposition. They were subject to an obedience that made them free, so content with their lot that it eventually became necessary to threaten with manumission any sky child guilty of any serious malfeasance; for to be given his 'freedom' was the most undesirable of fates. It would mean being left to fend for himself as best he could in the Valley, in whose history there have been only three cases of punitive manumission.

The older sky children, once they had passed beyond the stage where they could contribute productive labor, were settled upon small communal farms deep in the hills, where they were tendered those comforts which age requires. Fresh youths were commandeered to fill the labor pool, raiders being sent out periodically and of necessity farther and farther afield for the purpose of recruiting these youngsters.

The practice continued generation after generation, a practice whose survival depended of course upon maintaining the homogeneity of the landowners. Would-be settlers and land speculators were discouraged from crossing the Brokenstraw Range; some who ignored the legends that began to spread among the outsiders rashly came into the Valley and were never heard from again, so that the legends persisted, became more grisly and fanciful, until finally a wall of superstition higher than the tallest peak in the Brokenstraws ringed the Valley and barred all who would have entered uninvited.

Although I found much of what my father told me that day alarming and embarrassing, I don't recall finding it morally repugnant. My ethical sympathies were not engaged either on behalf of the sky children or of their masters. If, even now, you feel that I am playing too assiduously the role of devil's advocate, you must understand I do so in order to balance the bias which you, an outsider, must properly feel.

For you are the victim of your own value judgments. Your moral hackles rise at the sound or sight of the word *slave*, a word which connotes to you the most depraved and abominable of human conditions. You think of it instinctively in terms of whips and misery. You are blind to its philosophical justification—willfully blind, I might add, because there is a strong element of fear behind your value judgments of slavery. The arguments adduced by my father and which are today just as cogent to my nephews cannot be summarily dismissed except by the most shallow intelligence, for it is undeniably true that most people squander their gifts and waste their lives. They would be more happy if they were less free. Were my position based on the contradiction of that argument, it would be insupportable.

Intellectually, you see, I am in the devil's camp.

Nowhere will you find greater abundance and less waste than in this Valley, both of natural and human resources. However, the price for such abundance must be paid out of the soul, which soon becomes bankrupt. For those who enjoy this abundance and its fruits become monsters. Yes, the sky children are monsters, devoid of compassionate impulses, irredeemably selfish, because to them all is permitted. They fornicate at will, like animals, they eat and sleep and are content, subject only to that obedience which makes them free. And as for their masters, they, too, are monsters, enslaved by the traditional bonds of their responsibility to the sky children. They, too, are devoid of spiritual energy.

If you find it incredible that this exploitation of the sky children—or the exploitation of their masters *by* the sky children—should have been perpetuated into the middle of the present century, you must remember that we are still sequestered behind that wall of superstition which not even the bravest can penetrate without peril. And these legends of which I spoke, and with which mothers on the outskirts of the Valley still frighten their own children into obedience, are still fortified periodically by actual deeds, the bloody details of which even I, thank God, am ignorant.

After God's Angels enlightened me to the wickedness of this system, declaring it to be an affront to the Almighty, I wore myself out in appeals to Edward and Eldred, who had at their fingertips arguments which even my father had never thought of. If I pleaded for spiritual compassion, they blandly pointed out the happiness of the sky children. If I mentioned God's holy Name, they called Him the greatest slave holder of all time and the cruelest, demanding obedience and giving nothing in return but the dubious promise of eternal bliss. If I spoke of outrages against nature, they described the natural condition of mankind as being a balance of mastery and bondage, declaring that there are those with a psychic craving to dominate and those with an inborn urge to be dominated. They reminded me with scorn of the duplicity of modern moral standards in the outside world, where to forget oneself in the service of others is preached from every pulpit, but where none are held in such contempt as those who actually serve others.

Sometimes the Holy Voices are silent, and then I am beset by conflicting anxieties and almost believe that this agony of soul is no more than ethical confusion.

For a long time my nephew Eldred, with Edward's connivance, has been engaged in a variety of experiments, the exact nature of which I can only speculate upon, but which involve the use of drugs, hypnosis, and parapsychology.

The raids have become more numerous, extending far beyond the Valley, to Plampton and Scours and Meadowlark, even as far south as Preacher Creek.

God's voice, coming to me out of the clouds and from the lips of lilies, grows urgent. Why cannot He understand that I am truly helpless? Why did He choose me as His instrument when I am so weak and sick and alone?

In his twisted way, Eldred is a genius. He invented a flower that has no color and whose fragrance clouds the mind. It is called Solomon's Concubine.

It is all managed scientifically. They are put gently to sleep and never feel the branding iron. They are pampered with the choicest victuals and finest raiments. See how fondly they smile, breathing always the 'golden lotus dust.' And there is sex. Sex is the golden whip with which they are cajoled. While their masters are casebooks of neuroses, there is no such thing as a frustrated sky child. Every perversion is allowed, even encouraged. I have seen male sky children—husky, virile farm workers—clasping their fellows in the fields and shamelessly disporting, throwing off their garments and sharing the lewd, unnatural embraces of their own sex, and then at night lying as wantonly with females. Why should they surrender such a paradise, leave Eden to become poor, starving clodbusters bedeviled by sick children and unpaid bills and the bonds of conformist behavior?

Edward and Eldred have been at loggerheads for months over some issue which could have the most far-reaching results, depending upon whose will prevails. Edward's is the stronger, and therefore the more dangerous. In spite of this, perhaps because he is so much like my father, whom I loved, Edward has always been closer to my heart, if one can hold monsters in affection.

Yesterday I saw Jesus walking in the garden. He looked at the ground and wept. Had I been able to move, I would have flung myself to the ground and crawled to him on my knees. He did not look at me, yet I felt that He knew I was there.

The Angels come sometimes in the night and whisper outside the window. I hear their precious wings beating softly against the pane.

My nephews are monsters, but they are not fiends. Evil is not their business. They are fanatics, convinced of the righteousness of their cause. I know what they are planning to do. They—"

Peter broke off abruptly at a sudden noise from high up on the bank where he'd hidden the bike.

He sprang up in time to see two youths hauling the bike out of the sumacs. Too angry to be scared, he scrambled up the bank shouting at them, but by the time he got to the road one of them had already disappeared into the woods and the other was riding off at top speed in the direction of Brokenstraw, leaving Peter alone in a settling cloud of dust.

For several minutes, he was too upset to appreciate his predicament or even to wonder how the thieves had spotted the bike. When he did finally accept the fact that he was stranded in the middle of nowhere, he knew he had no choice but to start walking, and since he would never reach either Brokenstraw or the farm before nightfall, the only logical move was to go boldly back to the Abbey, explain that his bike had been swiped, and ask to be driven home, or rather ask to be allowed to call Krieg—he didn't want any more rides with Dr. El. No reason for them to be suspicious.

He was still clutching the letter, and now, having made up his mind what to do, he carefully refolded it and tucked it once more into his shoe, postponing any further perusal until he was safe at the farm. Then, trying hard to believe he had nothing to worry about, he started walking toward the park.

"Town boys, I've not a doubt," asserted Dr. El.

"We'll report it at once," agreed Edward. "Why don't I do that, El, while you take care of our young adventurer. He looks in need of refreshment."

"If you don't mind," said Peter, not sure if he was imagining the confidential byplay between the brothers, "I'd like to call Krieg first."

"Leave that to me, too," answered Edward. "Don't you worry about a thing."

"A cold glass of milk and a half hour's rest is what the doctor prescribes." Peter tried not to recoil too visibly from the damp squeeze of Dr. El's hand.

"But the reason I wanted to talk to Krieg—they don't know I was out riding. My aunt wouldn't like it. She—"

"Relax, dear boy. I shall be a master of diplomacy." Edward's flickering smile, showing little bright bits of teeth, was not reassuring.

Dr. El led Peter up the stairs to the same room he'd had during his visit. He hadn't recalled its being so gloomy. Dr. El gave his hand another limp squeeze. "Such a joy having you back, cherub. Dare one hope one was missed?"

Peter managed a sickly smile.

"Now off with your shoes and lie down." Peter balked. Dr. El looked stern. "Doctor's orders, cherub."

Peter bent down and fumbled with his laces.

"I'm more thirsty than tired. I could sure go for that cold milk."

It worked, and while Dr. El went off to get the milk Peter yanked off his shoe and transferred the letter to his back pocket. He was lying on the bed with his eyes dutifully shut when Dr. El came back.

"While you're drinking your milk, cherub, I shall go down and see how Eddie is doing with those phone calls. When you've drunk the whole glass, you must lie back and try to sleep."

Instead, Peter hurried to the door and peeked up and down the passage. Seeing no one, he was about to step out when a sudden wave of dizziness made him grab tight to the knob. Frightened, he crept back to the bed and lay down. Cold milk drunk too rapidly on a nervous stomach. He'd rest a while and then try again. The longer he lay there, however, the less inclined he felt to move, the easier it was to surrender to the warm dark current that flowed over him.

He slept.

Awake. But was he? His eyes were open and he felt awake, yet there were clouds of doubt, caused by something he didn't understand but which kept him motionless, like someone regaining consciousness after a fall and afraid to make a move for fear that numbness will change to lancing pain.

Something on the far horizon of his vision was disturbingly wrong; though curious, he didn't want to know what it was, so he kept his eyes fixed dully on a spot above the door, preferring not to shift his gaze to the door itself because then he would know for certain what he now only sensed was true, that the door was the wrong color, the door and the walls, too; white instead of dark-paneled as they should have been. He was similarly aware of a difference in the bed: it was smaller, had metal rails, stood higher off the floor, and was also white.

Too much to cope with, he drifted back into the more comforting shadows of an interior vision.

The next awakening was sudden, like a lurching stop in

a car in which he'd fallen asleep, and this time his senses were extraordinarily acute.

The room *was* white. The bed *was* different.

It was not the same room.

When he raised his head it was as heavy as a bag of cement. Why he should feel such distress at finding he was in pajamas puzzled him. What had become of his clothes? Socks, shirt ... pants!

Miss Celestia's letter!

Sky children.

Now his eyes skimmed over the room and he knew he was on the third floor, in Dr. El's dispensary. It flooded back: the stolen bike, Edward and Dr. El.

Cold milk.

Wobbly legged, he felt his way to the closet, found his clothes neatly arranged on hangers. He fished through the pockets.

Miss Celestia's letter was gone.

He was putting on his shoes when the door opened. Dr. El.

"Naughty cherub. Mustn't get out of bed. Oh, my, no."

Peter held tight to the shoe. "What am I here for?"

"You don't remember how sick you became?"

"You gave me a glass of milk. Cold milk."

"Which you drank much too fast. I should have watched you. You became violently ill. Your day's adventures have overtaxed you, cherub. Now let me help you back to beddy."

Peter hadn't either the strength or will to resist.

"They stole the bike. I tried—"

"Lie back. Don't talk."

"I've got to get back to the farm. Aunt Affie—"

"Has been notified. They were very worried. They've agreed you'll be better off here for a little while. Now swallow this pretty little capsule, and you'll soon be feeling better."

He slipped it deftly onto Peter's tongue and thrust a glass of water at him.

"Good cherub. Now lie down. Close your eyes."

Yes, he wanted to do that. The light bothered them and made him squint as if it were sun, but when he closed them he began to spin so rapidly that he had to grab the sheets to keep from spinning out of bed. When he opened his eyes, he cried out; it hurt so to look into that fiercely brilliant light, a hundred times brighter than before. Why, it wasn't even the same light! This one was ever so much bigger and was formed by concentric coils of glass tubing.

When he tried to get away from it, he found he couldn't move.

He was strapped down, stark naked.

That's when he screamed.

"Mother! Mother! Don't let them!"

Hands flew over his face and tape was pressed across his lips. He turned his head and saw them standing a few feet away.

Aunt Affie was there, and Dr. El, and Edward, and Weems. And Welcome! Dressed like a nurse.

They were all smiling, and the smiles were identical, like the regulation smile a choir wears just before it breaks into song.

Aunt Affie stepped toward him. "Why, honey, you're awake. Feel all right, darlin'?"

Her hand was on his forehead, cool as a mint leaf.

"Dr. El knows just what'll cure you. Be a good boy and do what Dr. El says."

Strapped down, did he have a choice?

Away she drifted, hands fluttering, disappearing through a vaporous wall without even the sound of a door closing.

As if this were a signal, the others crowded around the table and leered down at him, gloating over him with wolf-eyed pleasure. Welcome suddenly laughed, a rude, nasal squawk like an angry swan's.

"Look at the little simp now. Scared green! Go ahead. Do it to him. Make him hurt!"

Edward cleared his throat. "I'm not at all sure I should watch. I hate to see anyone suffer."

Peter's tongue felt swollen, choking his throat.

"Now stop that, Eddie. Both of you. Tormenting the poor boy."

"What are you waiting for?" hissed Welcome. "Do it to him!"

Edward bared his teeth to the gums. "Let's see if he's a *red-blooded* American boy."

"Now you *know* there's never any blood." Dr. El was pettish. "Not the way I do it."

"Then let's see if our presence *pains* him."

Weems watched silently.

"Light the tapers," said Dr. El. "I'm going to scrub."

Edward turned to Welcome. "Did you hear that? He's going to *scrub*. What a professional. Perhaps we should all *scrub*."

"Oh, shut your mouth, Eddie, and light the tapers."

"Ah, by all means, brother dear, the tapers."

Edward disappeared, returning a moment later with two enormous black onyx candlesticks holding tall white candles, one of which he placed on a table beside Peter's head, the other somewhere near his feet. He stood back, rubbing his hands.

"Well, light them, light them!" cried Dr. El.

Edward did so, but the flames were quite lost under those dazzling overhead lights.

Peter's body seemed one huge throbbing heart. From somewhere nearby he heard running water. With tight shut eyes he tried desperately to frame a prayer, knowing it was hopeless, too late for deliverance.

A movement on his other side just as he opened his eyes. Dr. El's face, radiant, his pale, wizard's hand reaching across the table above Peter's chest.

"Iron," he said softly.

Peter's glance streaked to the other side; a convulsive quiver snaked across his skin as he saw Welcome hand Dr. El a silver branding iron, its white-hot tip a perfect star.

His bones dissolved; tears streamed from his eyes.

Welcome hooted. "Look at him blubber. Look!"

Edward said, "He knows we mean business." Then he leaned closer until his smoky-looking face with its polished eyes was almost directly over Peter's head. "You wanted to know all about the sky children, did you? Well, we're going to do better than that, sonny boy. We're going to let you join them. How do you like that?"

The tears kept flowing. Welcome rejoiced. "I don't think he likes it."

"Well, let him bawl his little head off, my dear. It won't do him any good now."

"His leg, Welcome, if you please."

Welcome seized Peter's right leg by the thigh and twisted it outward, causing the strap to bite into his ankle. Dr. El bent forward and rubbed the exposed area between Welcome's hands with a liquid that stung like dry ice. Peter shuddered, strove mightily to break the straps pinning him to the table.

"Hold his noggin, Eddie!" ordered Dr. El, and Edward moved around the table behind Peter, placed his hands on each side of Peter's head, and tilted it backward in a fleshy vise.

It was unnecessary, for as soon as Peter saw the branding iron begin its maddeningly slow arc, he again clamped his lids tight together and held his breath, praying he would black out before the iron touched him. His will was not strong enough; he gave an involuntary gasp.

Still the brand hovered; in every throbbing nerve he could feel it poised above him.

Dr. El whispered in his ear. "Hotter it is the less it hurts, cherub."

Edward said, "It won't hurt for long, will it, El?"

"Oh, not for *very* long."

The tension passed the humanly bearable point, and Peter vomited through his nose.

"Welcome!" It was the shrilly demonic voice Peter had heard on the ridge above the Breed graveyard. "The little snot's puked over everything!"

"Burn him for it!" she shrieked.

"Clean it up. Hurry!"

"Filthy little beast."

Peter groaned as his face was roughly wiped with a damp cloth, twisting his body as far as he could under the restraining straps, while Edward held tight to his head. There was a smell of disinfectant.

"Oh, for God's sake, El, get it over with!" cried Edward.

"If you're going to puke, brother dear, please have the decency to do it outside."

"I just wish you'd hurry up, that's all."

"One doesn't rush a *ritual*."

"He's turning a funny shade of green, Doctor," observed Welcome.

"Put this over his eyes," said Dr. El, and Peter felt something like heavy flannel laid across his face.

"But now he can't see it," pouted Welcome.

"We don't want him passing out, do we?"

A moment of silence, and then she said, "Oooooo ... hotsy-totsy!"

"Want your hair singed?" giggled Dr. El.

And now he knew it was going to happen; he couldn't hear the respiration of a single breath.

Mother! Daddy! Jesus!

"Now!" cried Dr. El.

Pain, though not what he had expected; so swift, clean, and sharp it might have been no more than the injection of a needle; he couldn't believe it was over and he was still rigid, still waiting, when his mind began drifting away ...

The ceiling was swarming with bees; he could see them crawling out of dark holes and gathering in clusters around the enormous circular tubes of light above his head until they were so thick the light was completely obscured and the room dark as night and the bees began emitting sparks that were brightly colored, purple and green and gold and blue.

Outside the window the trees were perfectly still, not a leaf stirring; very odd, uncanny, considering how fiercely the wind was blowing.

After this only partial awakenings, brief, groping, followed by another deeper plunge; always the sparkling kinetic darkness, sound of bees; always the wind, wild and howling but tame, as in a bottle or shell; exploding flowers, sometimes in a room as small as a coffin or a shoebox, or big as the railway station at home.

The sun beating against the closed blind made a peculiar swishing noise, tempting him out of bed and across the room. The floor seemed not quite even and he almost slipped a couple of times as if he were crossing glare ice. Raising the blind, he felt the golden impact of the sun.

It was morning. No, afternoon.

The garden below was a huge pit of blazing flowers encircled by a golden haze.

One good thing; he was in the right room at last. Warm, dark walls. Four-poster bed.

The door opened softly and Aunt Affie peeked in. She saw he was up, smiled, stepped in, all fuss and fingers.

He stared at her very coldly.

"Why'd you let them do it?"

The hanky with which she tapped her nose had a finely tatted border. "Do what, darlin'?"

"Brand me."

The words came before the recollection and for the first time his fingers traveled gingerly to the spot, felt beneath the cotton pajamas a bulky bandage.

She swiftly crossed the room, grabbed his hand away from the spot. "Come back to bed. You'll get dizzy and fall."

"I'm not dizzy. Leave me alone!" Which wasn't quite the truth, nor quite a lie, either; this odd feeling wasn't exactly dizziness.

"Why, Peter Patrick . . ." Her face was wounded, lugubrious.

"You *let* them! I'm getting out of here and I'm going to tell Mother and Daddy all about it. I'm going to tell them everything. Just because they stole the letter—"

"Hush now, sweetheart." A smile crept sinuously around her face. "Are those nasty old thieves after you again? Shame on them."

"It's not funny! And this isn't, either." He started to undo his pajamas to get at the bandage, but she stopped him by throwing her arms around him and urging him toward the bed.

"Mustn't touch that bandage. Dr. El had to do that."

"While you stood there and let him."

"Why, what's gotten into you? 'Course I let him. I came soon as they called and told me how sick you were."

"But you let them do *that!*"

"Darlin', when somebody's as sick as you were and they can't be sure what's wrong, it's customary to draw blood for a blood test."

Her look of phony innocence maddened him. "Why are you *lying?*"

"Peter, darlin'—"

"Why are you pretending? Why are you trying to get me all mixed up?"

Not even Gram could have worn such a soulful look. "You are a tiny bit mixed up, sweetheart. But don't worry. Crisis is past. You're goin' to be all well again."

"I haven't been sick! I was riding my bike yesterday—"

"Not yesterday, sweet. Last Wednesday."

Speechless, he squirmed beneath her gently compassionate gaze.

"Now, I know you're still unwell, Peter, and I shall make allowances. We all shall. But you must try to help us."

"You're saying things. Why are you—"

"You've been punished enough, darlin', for breakin' the rules. I'm not goin' to say no more about that, 'cept that we made them rules for your own good. When you deliberately broke them and went flyin' off on your cousin's wheels without so much as an aye-yes-or-no to anyone, you was only hurtin' yourself. Ridin' so far in the heat. If they hadn't found you layin' there in the road when they did, well . . ." She ended with a portentous shake of the head.

"It wasn't like that at all. Who told you that?"

"Why, Mr. Breed, of course."

"He lied! Two boys, they stole the bike—"

"Honey, honey. Luke's wheels is right downstairs. You can see for yourself soon's you're all better. You're just a wee bit hazy 'bout things yet. Don't you see? That's what fever can do."

She turned to the table. "Now you're up and awake, you can drink your milk and eat your oatmeal. You must be famished, ain't you, darlin'? Here. Maybe I better feed you . . ."

He grabbed the spoon away from her. "I'm quite able to feed myself, thank you."

He was indeed hungrier than he'd ever been in his life. The oatmeal slid down, and then the milk. He burped noisily and lay back on the pillow.

"Where's Krieg?"

"You'll see him later."

"It wasn't his fault, you know."

"Well . . ." Her tone was very damaging to Krieg.

"I gave him the slip. He couldn't help it."

"Lay down, honey."

"Don't go away."

"I'm right here."

But she wasn't.

Blurry, colorless clouds were covering her; she was barely visible. He could no longer hold the glass and had to set it down with excessive care that it shouldn't fall and break, while Aunt Affie kept receding until she was as small as a common pin, then gone.

And in her place the bees, the wind, exploding flowers.

As a precisely calculable medium, time had ceased to exist, a fact causing him no anxiety whatsoever; on the contrary, it was a big relief, giving him an extraordinary sense of freedom. Time's unclocked hours let him roam at will into the corridors of the past as if it were another wing of the Abbey, contiguous to the one he was in, though not so well lighted, making it necessary to feel his way among shapes definable enough but webbed with shadows that were curiously tactile.

Once, looking down into the garden, he wondered if this was what it meant to be one of the sky children. When he was well, would they give him certain tasks to do? What would he be suited for? A sort of page or minor flunky, perhaps.

Or Dr. El's apprentice?

The wizard's apprentice.

Terror seized hold of him whenever he spoke to someone or touched something, because there was this queer sensation that another Peter Patrick, himself but not him*self*, stood between him and the other person or thing, that he himself was not the real Peter Patrick but only a shadow or *doppelgänger* who would eventually fade entirely from the scene, fade away and cease to be, and it was this vagueness of being that made him so frightfully insecure.

He felt neither regret nor relief when Dr. El drove him back to the farm, didn't know in fact that he was going back there when they started out.

"Anything planned for the day, cherub?"

He assumed he was accompanying Dr. El on his rounds when they started out, and he seemed to know by a kind of extended *déjà vu* exactly what roads they would take, at what farms they would stop, how the people would look, and so he was mildly baffled when they ended up at Sugar Hill instead.

"You look ever so much better," chirped Welcome, planting a chaste, dry kiss on his suddenly cold cheek.

"I'm okay," he said, and it was as if someone else a few feet away were actually speaking the words in a voice that was hollow and unreal.

"Guess what," she said. "They're having a welcome home party for you."

"This isn't my home," the Voice said.

"Mrs. Juul wants me to make rosettes. You can help, lovey."

He thought of the hot iron and heard the Voice scream.

He wondered where they could be taking him in his bathrobe and slippers in the middle of the night. Aunt Affie was on one side and Welcome on the other. He hadn't been out since coming back to the farm, and that was— when? A few minutes ago? Yesterday? Last week? It was all the same.

"Where are we going?"

"To see Krieg."

At last!

"Where is he?"

"In the barn."

Why should he have to go to the barn to see Krieg?

He stopped, charmed almost to tears by the sweet meadow air and the moon gliding above the pines.

He had been in the barn many times, of course, but it looked different with all those benches lined up in front of a platform laid across several big sawhorses, and why were all these people here?

Edward and Dr. El. Theron and Cleo. Mr. Lipscomb. Old MacSorley and a score of people he'd never seen before. They were all murmuring sociably but quietly, like people in church before the service begins.

Settled between Welcome and Aunt Affie on one of the back benches, he pulled at Aunt Affie's sleeve and asked where Krieg was and why all these people were here.

Welcome giggled. "It ain't no Sunday auction, lovey."

"You'll see Krieg any minute now," said Aunt Affie.

He didn't bother asking why one of the men was going around extinguishing the lanterns. By the time there was only one left burning near the door, the crowd had become very quiet.

A man came onto the platform and threw a thick rope up over one of the crossbeams. He failed to reach it the first three tries. Each time it fell back to the platform, the people on the benches chuckled, and when he finally did make it, there was a smattering of applause.

He fashioned a noose on the end of the rope.

It was very dark up by the roof. Peter remembered something about being hidden in a barn loft. Who was it who'd told him about that? Being hidden in a barn loft and overhearing terrible things.

Terrible things.

Terrible things were happening right here and now, he could feel it and he wanted to get away, but the moment he stirred Welcome and Aunt Affie moved closer, pinning him between them.

Edward Breed stood facing them up there on the platform. His attitude was ministerial, as he made quieting motions with his fat white hands, baring his teeth in a sanctimonious leer.

"You all know why we've been assembled here this evening. One among us has been charged with gross neglect of duty, has been convicted of this charge and has had sentence imposed upon him. Herewith let that sentence be carried out."

He stepped off the platform and rejoined Dr. El on the front bench.

Had Peter been able to move he would have jumped to his feet when he saw two men come out of the shadows at the rear of the platform, for Krieg was between them.

He was naked and his wrists were bound together.

The one remaining lantern must have been turned down, for the figures on the platform became mere shadows enacting a macabre ballet of movements during which the noose was fitted around Krieg's neck and the two husky giants took hold of the other end of the rope and, as the light faded to a blood-red glow, strained to hoist Krieg's shadow-body from the floor.

Peter was led away screaming.

He was afraid to look at the flowers, geraniums, for when geraniums exploded it was hell to watch. He looked upward at the wind chimes instead, those delicate splinters of painted glass tinkling up there below the cornice, scarcely moving in the raging wind, no more than a breath would move them.

"Time for your pill, darlin'."

Aunt Affie in a daisied apron. Docile as a tame bird, he gulped down the capsule, drank the water, and then forced himself to look at the geraniums, blood-bright in yellow porch boxes. He could almost feel the pill disintegrating, making its swift insidious way into his bloodstream, and soon now, very soon—

"Peter!"

He looked at her.

"Peter, what's the matter with you?"

"Nothing."

"Now don't tell me that. You haven't heard a single word I've been saying to you."

He supposed if he took the trouble, he could tell how soon it happened after the ingestion of a pill.

Aunt Affie looked grieved, sounded put upon. "I should think you'd be thrilled to pieces."

A pinhead bubble of blood oozed from the cuticle of his thumb where he couldn't stop biting it.

"Shame it had to end like this. We all had such hopes."

He sucked the blood away, bound his handkerchief so tightly around the tiny lesion his whole thumb began to throb.

"If only you hadn't took sick. But you did enjoy bein' here, didn't you, darlin'? 'Course you did. And I know you'll feel like a million dollars again when they get here. Right about now that old train ought to be pullin' into Plato Switch ... Peter?"

"Hmmm?"

"You listenin' to me?"

He nodded vaguely, his attention riveted on the geraniums. A small brown spider was crawling out of one of them. If it didn't hurry ...

"Peter, what's *wrong* with you?"

"They're going to explode."

"What?"

"Blow up!"

"What in tarnation you talkin' about?"

"The geraniums."

"Here, let me feel of you. Maybe you better go in and lay down—"

"No!"

"Honey—"

"They don't fool me, you know. Those pills."

"Now you're not going to get yourself into a state just when your folks are almost here, are you? They're worried enough as it is."

He glared at her with truly savage hatred. "Just wait till I tell them!"

He didn't hear her reply, because just as she opened her mouth the fireworks began, tight red blossoms bursting into gigantic lurid fireballs, gaudy scarlet torches so fiercely brilliant the air around them went gray as dusk.

The ceiling was alive with them—buzz, buzz, buzz—and the wind, without so much as stirring the curtains at the open window, still sounded capable of smashing the house like an eggshell. Wax begonias shot spikes of frozen fire into the/half-light of his room.

Always after a capsule, or after he'd eaten something, or had a drink of water. He knew perfectly well what would happen, but he took them anyway. He hadn't the will to resist.

He tried not to believe he didn't *want* to resist.

It would be all right once he'd talked to Mother and Daddy. Then he could stop playing this crazy game with them. His fingers strayed over the old suitcase.

Non ignara mali.

He began to cry because he didn't really believe they were coming, or that he would ever see them again.

Another hallucination, he thought at first, having never, even on the clearest day, heard the sound of churchbells. The steeple of the simple country church at Brokenstraw was a familiar sight; on many of his rambles with Krieg he had seen it shining, a silver needle against the far horizon. Now, from his window, he distinctly heard the measured tolling which could be issuing only from its bell, a somber but infinitely comforting sound which he could have listened to forever. It cast a spell of dream-deep silence over misty pond and Fragonard-like trees, and the silver-green sky of dusk.

The bell seemed to draw him down the stairs and out onto the porch where he came upon Cleo standing alone on the top step, looking out across the meadows toward Brokenstraw, as if she, too, were entranced.

"Why are they ringing it?" he asked her, and she looked at him absently, slack-lipped, and said, "For Miss Celestia."

"But why?"

"She's dead."

A shiver speared him, and the bell had suddenly a piercing, throat-clutching, heart-stopping resonance. A bird—no doubt a robin, but looking very black against the fading sky—soared in a wide rising arc above the elms, flapped its wings but twice, as if the air were so pure and buoyant it took no effort at all to move upon it.

"So they killed her, too," he said bitterly.

Cleo shrugged, still looking a long way off, her spindly fingers pressed against the yellow pillar. "Don't be silly," she said.

He wanted to say something about Krieg, if only it weren't so impossible to frame his name; he tried, but then the bell would toll and sweep it, quivering, from his lips, unsaid.

"How can you stay here?"

She didn't look around. "What do you mean?"

"You loved him."

Her indifference maddened him. She was like a zombie. Well, wasn't he, too? Two zombies conversing in a dead language, uttering sounds without meaning. Not even signals.

"I know you did. I saw you together."

"Did you?"

"The day Krieg picked me up at the station. I saw you in the woods."

"Poor boy. Always seeing things."

"You loved him. And you watched him die."

"Always seeing things," she said again, making it sound like the most dismal kind of truth.

"You just sat there and didn't even try to stop it."

"Stop an illusion?"

"Death?"

Each of them spoke swiftly, squeezing their words between the tollings of the bell.

"Death. Love. Illusions."

"The sky children? Illusion, too?"

She waited three strokes of the bell before speaking. Then, looking up; "All of it. Everything. Even the sky . . . it's not really there . . . oh, God, how awful . . . the sky is not *there!*"

He looked up at it, for only an instant.

She said very slowly, "All that blue . . . nothing!"

For the length of a breath, not even that long, he understood Cleo, saw beyond the thin, proud lips, beneath the purple surface of her eyes, even a glimpse of her heart, who she was, what she was, maybe even why, a momentary revelation that disturbed him because he was satisfied with the image he already had of her. And what she said about the sky pricked some ancient, unacknowledged, prenatal, tribal fear, and he said quickly, "How long will they keep ringing it?"

"*Tolling.* Bells *ring* only on happy occasions. This is not a happy occasion."

"Do you care—that she's dead?"

"Yes."

Liar!

"Why?"

"You wouldn't understand."

The view before them, the sky, the bell, her very bearing gave her the aura and glamour of an authentic oracle, the sibyl of Sugar Hill.

"I understand more than you think I do."

She favored him with a smile as wry as Cassandra's. "Most folks think if you don't believe in one thing, you must believe in the other. Fools."

This was too cryptic for him.

But she was right about the sky.

He would have screamed it if he dared, but it wouldn't make any difference.

"Yes, Peter," she kept saying. "Yes, Peter. Now do hurry. We have to be at the station in an hour or we'll miss the train."

That they had actually arrived, both of them, Mother and Daddy, fretful as ever and so completely normal, was both incredible and gladdening, but now this stupid inability to understand what he kept telling them was killing his joy.

"Mother, *listen* ... Daddy!"

Daddy's mouth formed a tight white line under his skimpy moustache, which might have been pasted on, looking as spurious, in fact, as the reasonable expression in the pale blue eyes above it. "All right, young man, we've heard enough."

"Don't scold him, Daddy. He's a very sick boy." She smoothed Peter's sun-bleached hair away from his forehead, gazed at him adoringly. "Angel, you must understand that when you have a fever you have—well, they're like waking dreams. Your mind plays funny little tricks on you."

Funny little tricks!

"They were all in on it. I saw the scars and found out about the sky children."

Daddy was about to say something but Mother gave him a look, so all he did was purse his lips.

And now the proof. He had been right to delay, to hold back the unveiling even from his own eyes. Let them explain this!

"Look." The drawstring was knotted, and it took suspensefully longer than he'd planned to loosen his pajamas.

"That's a good boy, angel," said Mother, mistaking the action. "Get dressed now, quickly."

"I want you to see this. I told you what they did. Now I can show you the proof. Help me with this darned knot!"

Mother gently pulled his hands away and easily undid the knot. He shoved her away and pulled his pajamas down, unmindful of his nakedness.

It was going to hurt like blazes, and he knew this was one of the reasons he hadn't wanted to remove the bandage earlier. Stripping that adhesive tape from the skin would be agony.

Non ignara mali.

It stung like fire.

"Look!—"

Beneath the bandage the white, puckered skin revealed nothing but a minuscule puncture mark.

His mother's voice sounded so gentle it might have been coming from another room, or world. "Angel, Dr. Eldred explained that. He had to take a blood sample. You made such a fuss. You imagined things. He thought it best to bandage it. Now you've only excited yourself needlessly, and that's not good for you. Daddy and I will help you get dressed."

So monumental was his fatigue his tongue itself hung limply in his mouth, and it was not until they had nearly finished dressing him, shifting his arms and legs about as if he were a doll, that he could spur himself to a final effort.

"They murdered Krieg."

"Daddy, help him with that sleeve."

"I said they *murdered* Krieg!"

"Not so loud, angel. They'll hear you downstairs."

"THEY MURDERED KRIEG! THEY HANGED HIM IN THE BARN!"

Mother winced.

Daddy's face got red. "Listen to me, young man. If I hear any more of this rubbish—"

"Charles! He is *sick*. Can't you get that through your head?"

"Never mind *my* head. It's *his* you'd better start worrying about."

While they were squabbling Peter finished dressing himself, and when he'd put his pajamas and brush and comb in the suitcase he made a last-minute search of the empty drawers.

"What are you looking for, angel?"

"The letter."

"What letter?"

Daddy said, "You'd better make it snappy. It's time we got started."

"What letter, angel?"

"Miss Celestia's. She had it all written down. You might believe her even if you don't believe me. But they stole it. I know it's not here."

"Miss Celestia's being buried today," Mother said. "If we didn't have to catch the train, we could all go to the funeral. Just as well, I guess. It might upset you more."

"But she depended on me to stop them. She trusted me."

"Now, angel, you know that Miss Breed was a very old lady. Even older than Gram. You remember what Gram was like, don't you, toward the end? How she imagined all those things. Heard voices and saw things that weren't there ..."

Did it really matter any more? Miss Celestia was dead, and he was getting out of there, going home, so why make any fuss? Forget it. Pretend it was all a dream.

And yet ... murder.

"You're going to let them get away with murder?"

"Peter, Peter ..."

"I swear on the Bible, cross my heart and hope to die—"

"Don't say that!" Mother's voice was on the ragged edge now.

Daddy said, "Can he put his shoes on, or is he going to wear those slippers all the way home?"

"Angel, where are your shoes? Take your slippers off and get your shoes on. It's getting late."

"I'm telling you about a murder, a cold-blooded murder, and you talk about slippers!"

"I *said* that's enough, young man."

He let them help him downstairs.

Aunt Affie was waiting for them on the porch, the others having all gone to the funeral. She handed Mother a box lunch for them to eat on the train.

"Just some cold chicken and a few egg salad sandwiches. Hold it careful now, don't squeeze it, there's some rosettes in there, too." She looked at Peter as she said this, twinkling her eyes to make her look like Gram, which no longer fooled Peter now that he knew she had all the tricks of a witch up her sleeve. He shied away when she bent to kiss him.

"Peter!" cried Mother. "Be nice."

"I do hope and pray he'll be all right. And I'm sure he will once he gets home. He's such a sweetheart; you've no idea how much I'm going to miss him."

Witch.

Mother chattered on about how much she appreciated all Aunt Affie had done and promising to keep her informed of Peter's progress. Daddy had carried the suitcase downstairs, and now Peter was looking about uneasily, wondering who was going to take them to the station.

Maybe they weren't going after all.

He didn't like the look on Aunt Affie's face. It wasn't at all like Gram's now: there was a curious, sly eagerness about it.

While they were still talking, Peter glanced down the drive and saw the old Willys appear, gleaming as though freshly waxed for the occasion, and then, as reflected images slid off the windshield and he could see through it, his legs almost buckled beneath him.

Krieg was behind the wheel!

He stepped out as nimbly as ever and carried Peter's suitcase from the porch to the car.

"You're sure you're okay?" Daddy said to Krieg, with a satirical side glance at Peter.

Krieg winked at Peter. "Yes, sir. I'm fine."

"One would have thought resurrection might involve a certain amount of fatigue."

The last good-byes were said, and they got in the car.

"Come again next year," called Aunt Affie. "All of you. For a nice vacation."

"Maybe we will," Mother promised, holding the box lunch carefully in her lap.

Once they were on their way, Daddy did most of the talking, but when he started to make another joke about

Krieg's miraculous return to life, Mother cut him off. "Let's just forget all that, shall we?"

Daddy grunted. "Fine by me. I just want to be sure Peter realizes how absurd all that rubbish was. You do, don't you, son?"

"It was true. All of it."

Daddy's face got pink. He was sitting up front with Krieg, and when he turned his head his profile was sharp and hard. "Oh, use your head. You told us this young man had been strung up in some barn. Who's driving us to the station—a ghost?"

Peter didn't answer.

When they got to the station it was deserted except for the stationmaster in his alcove by the window. Peter gave a start when he saw him. The man turned. It wasn't the same one. This was a younger man who gave them a brief, amiable nod.

Krieg insisted on shaking hands with Peter. Peter's eyes were fixed on his in silent, urgent entreaty. But Krieg merely took his hand away, saluted Mother and Daddy with a smart nod, and turned away.

Peter watched him till he was out of sight, hoping he would at least turn around and wave.

But he didn't.

"What are they waiting for?" he cried peevishly. His head throbbed and he could hardly breathe in the stifling air, even with the window open.

"One of the passengers, I guess."

"Where's Daddy gone?"

"He'll be right back."

Several minutes passed before the whistle sounded and Peter saw Daddy coming down the aisle, a newspaper under his arm, and followed by a woman whom Peter couldn't see clearly until Daddy had sat down in the seat across the aisle and two seats ahead of his and Mother's.

The woman sat down beside Daddy. Peter was conscious of a dreadful falling sensation.

It was Welcome!

Before sliding into the seat she fluttered her fingers at Peter and gave him her old familiar valentine smile.

Aghast, he whispered to Mother, "What's *she* doing here?"

"Not so loud, angel."

"What's she on the train for?"

With a look of inner satisfaction which appalled Peter, she said, "If you must know, dear, she's going to come home with us for a while."

This mild reply had the same shrinking effect on his body as would a blast of icy air through the window. "What for?"

"Well, Aunt Affie insisted. Until you're better, Welcome's going to look after you and help me with the housework." Suddenly she ducked her head and gave him a secret, dazzling smile. "And what's more, my angel, it's not going to cost us a red cent!"

His cold fingers dug into her arm. "But, Mother, she's one of *them!*"

She thrust her head away from him. "Now, Peter, cut that out. And let go of me. That hurts."

The hills were closing in upon the tracks, still dense, but with lighter shades of green and russet mottling the deeper greens and blues as the pines became sparser and the deciduous forest began.

"Mother, you've got to listen to me. You can't let her come home with us."

Fine lines of irritation threatened to demolish the patient serenity of her expression, though her voice remained gentle. "Well, she *is* coming home with us. And don't start anything or your father will hit the ceiling. He's fed up with your stories as it is. And I can't altogether blame him." Then her voice turned wistful, cajoling, as if she were trying to communicate some personal vision which she knew he couldn't possibly share. "Think how nice it will be, angel. A maid. *We'll* have a maid! I can't wait to see Alice Lynch's face when she finds out. And I don't want you to breathe a word to anybody, especially Teddy and Sue Ann, about why she's with us."

"Who's going to pay her?" he asked nastily.

"Aunt Affie. She absolutely insisted. She feels partly to blame for your being sick."

"No kidding!"

"Well, she isn't, I know that. But she's a dear old soul, and I only wish I'd had time to sit down and reminisce with her about Gram and Aunt Abigail and Uncle Roy. You don't remember them." Her eyes became faintly glazed with pleasure. "A maid. Just think. I can't get over it. *Us* with a maid."

It was pointless to argue; nobody would listen to him; nobody would believe him. Every so often he would throw covert glances across the aisle where Welcome's valentine smile was beamed at Daddy, and Daddy was talking animatedly.

Presently, he nudged Mother.

"What is it, angel?"

"Look at them."

She followed his eyes. "What about them?"

"Can't you see the way she's looking at Daddy?"

"I don't know what you mean."

"The way she's *looking* at him."

"Oh, Peter, what a funny boy you are."

He was trying meanwhile to reconstruct Miss Celestia's letter from memory, searching for a clue to what it was Edward and Dr. El were planning to do which had so alarmed her, vaguely recalling an argument the brothers had had one night at the dinner table, something to do with Azariah Breed's journals, some dispute about carrying or spreading or expanding something beyond the Ridge. . . .

A sickening apprehension fastened upon his mind as he continued to watch Welcome and Daddy.

"Mother, you've got to make her go back!"

She looked him straight in the eye with frank annoyance. "Don't talk silly, Peter."

"But I know all about her. I know why they've sent her. I know what she's up to."

"My dear, deluded child, Aunt Affie is the soul of respectability. She's employed that girl for years. So let's hear no more of this nonsense."

He looked backward out the window, as if the train had carried him to a distant enough point where destiny's precise shape and pattern could be seen with astonishing clarity of vision.

Now he knew why they had let him come to Brokenstraw in the first place, why they had kept him, and why they were now sending him away: all part of a plot whose far-reaching monstrous complexity might be infinitely more sinister than he imagined.

Looking back, he wondered now if Miss Celestia had been the most pitiful victim of the plot or the most diabolical of the conspirators. Phrases from her letter came back to him, phrases that seemed to echo Dr. El's very words. Perhaps he had even composed it!

One thing alone was clear: they had used him; he had served their purpose.

He wished he could hear what they were talking about over there. Whatever Welcome had just said had brought a pinkish blush to Daddy's face. Daddy rarely blushed.

The train rumbled on, chugging to a grinding jerky stop at various hamlets, where there would be a noisy metallic clatter as milk cans were trundled onto the train from the platforms.

Presently, Peter began to squirm with discomfort.

"I want my pills," he said.

Mother looked at her watch. "It's only seven o'clock."

"I want them *now*."

"Angel, please don't be difficult—"

"*Now!*"

She went out and got a paper cup of water.

He swallowed both pills, telling himself he wouldn't take any more of them once he got home. No matter how much he wanted them, he would resist the craving.

About a half hour later, he pinched Mother's arm. She gave a faint cry. "Peter, I thought you were asleep. You've been quiet as a mouse."

"I've been watching them."

She didn't answer. He said, "Look at them now, Mother."

Her voice was strained. "Well, what about them?"

"See how she's looking at Daddy."

"I don't know what you mean, I'm sure."

"The way she's *looking* at him."

Mother stared at him, instead, and this time there was more than just mild astonishment in her expression. "Peter Patrick! Do you by any chance mean what I think you mean?"

His voice rang with triumph, as if he had finally taught the blind to see. "Yes!"

She looked quite shattered. "What a nasty, filthy thing to say. A boy your age. You ought to be ashamed."

And then, returning her bored and absent gaze to the dismal, hot, somber, flattening countryside, she added mechanically, "I'd certainly like to know what you've been up to this summer."